Eve didn't know w[...]
at that point that the fog descended over her, and she ran out of the auditorium under its protective cover.

How could she go into the theater tomorrow after school as if nothing had happened, she wondered. She couldn't face them—any of them. Especially Miss Raden. But she couldn't let them down either. The play was in two weeks. More importantly, she couldn't let herself down. Somehow she would go in there, and she would play her part so well that everyone would forget she even had a father. Because that's exactly what she intended to do. Wipe him out of her mind and out of her life—forever.

I'm an orphan she thought. I'm on my own.

Also by Marilyn Levy
Published by Fawcett Juniper Books:

THE GIRL IN THE PLASTIC CAGE

LIFE IS NOT A DRESS REHEARSAL

LOVE IS A LONG SHOT

SUMMER SNOW

KEEPING SCORE

TOUCHING

Marilyn Levy

FAWCETT JUNIPER • NEW YORK

RLI: VL: 6 & up
    IL: 7 & up

A Fawcett Juniper Book
Published by Ballantine Books
Copyright © 1988 by Marilyn Levy

ISBN 0-449-70267-7

Printed in Canada

First Edition: May 1988

Thanks to Andrea, Tracy, Angel, Chris, and the kids at Clare.

Chapter One

"The place looks great," Eve said, looking around the living room.

"I was hoping you'd come back," her father said, smiling tentatively at her. "It's been like this all week."

Sure, it has, Eve thought, wondering where he had stashed the empty beer cans and vodka bottles.

"They're not here," her father said, watching her closely. "I've been sober since the day after you left. I'm going to stay that way."

"I've heard that one before," she said softly, looking away from him as he tried to maintain the smile on his craggy face, shaven so clean she could see light blue veins under his ruddy, weathered skin. He cleared his throat once and looked down at his feet. She looked at him hard. His dark hair was turning gray. She had never noticed that before. And the smile lines and dimple lines around his mouth were creased so heavily they looked like ridges some long-forgotten sled had made in the snow. He looked down again and shuffled his feet from one uncomfortable position to another. She felt sorry for him. He looked so vulnerable, as if he didn't know quite what to say or do.

She turned away. She didn't want to feel sorry for him. She wanted to look up to him, respect him, think he was the most wonderful father in the world. She wanted to love him as she used to when she was a little kid. Before he started drinking.

She touched the cast that covered her broken arm. She wanted to remember why she had left home in the first place. She wanted to remember what he was like when he wasn't sober. She wanted to remember how she felt when he had chased her out of the house after Binnie's birthday party.

The one thing she didn't want to do was let herself be taken in again. She stiffened her back against him and started walking toward her room. Let him work out his problems himself. She was sick of taking care of him. She wanted someone to take care of her.

"Your room is all fixed up," he said. "I didn't really touch anything. I just kind of straightened it up, vacuumed, picked up all the clothes lying around. I hope you don't mind," he added.

She couldn't stand it. He was trying so hard to please her. She hated seeing him like this. It was almost worse than seeing him passed out, dead drunk.

"I'm not staying," she said without looking at him. "I just came back to get some stuff I need for school." She didn't want to tell him why she had really come back. Why bother? Why upset him all over again? She knew this was hard enough on him. She had no interest in seeing him suffer. She just wanted to get her things and get out as quickly as she could so she could breathe again. The air in the room suddenly seemed very thin, and her shallow breathing hurt her chest.

"Things will be different this time," he said quickly. "I promise."

"No," she said, standing in front of her door. "They won't be different." They'll be terrific for a few days, and then something will happen to set him off again, and it'll be just like it always is, she thought. "Delphi's mom said I could stay there for as long as I want. It'll be better that way."

There was a long, nerve-racking pause. She looked around her room trying to locate her juggling balls as quickly as possible. She hadn't taken them with her when she left because she didn't think she'd have much use for them with a broken arm. But she missed them. They were her security blanket. Maybe she could learn to juggle with one hand.

She walked over to her dresser where she usually kept them. They weren't there. She could feel the anger growing inside her stomach like some fierce jungle cat ready to leap at its prey. *He* took them. She knew it. He hated to watch her juggle. Said it made him nervous. She knew that wasn't the reason. He hated anything that had to do with entertainment. Oh, it was all right as long as someone else was doing the entertaining, but he couldn't stand the thought of her standing in front of an audience doing her tricks. And she was good too. All her friends said so. They loved to watch her. She could juggle anything. She could balance anything. Even a stool on the bridge of her nose.

But she was sure he had thrown them away while she was gone. If he thought this would make her want to come home, he was really stupid on top of everything else.

She spun around to accuse him.

"Look in the box on your nightstand," he said before she could say anything.

She didn't move. The angry cat inside her scratched at her. It had leaped into her throat, constricting it so that she couldn't talk. She was just waiting for it to lose its footing and slip back down to her stomach so she could tell her father just how unbelievably cruel he was. Those were *her* special juggling balls, the ones her mother had given to her before—

He walked over to the nightstand and picked up a white box tied together with a huge, red ribbon, like a birthday present. Some toy, no doubt, to buy her off as he used to when she was little. Some furry brown bear or calico cat to put on her bed. Well, she wasn't a kid anymore, and he couldn't buy her off with presents this time.

He picked up the box and tried to hand it to her. She just stared at him, her gray eyes red with hatred.

He untied the ribbon, put it down on the dresser, took off the top of the box, and reached inside.

She turned away. This was pathetic. She didn't even care what was inside the box. Whatever it was it couldn't make up for the loss of her special juggling balls.

She heard the box drop to the floor.

Her father cleared his throat again. "The salesman said these were the best ones in the store. 'Primo,' he said. 'She'll love 'em.' "

She looked up to see just what he was going on about. Piled into his hands was the juggling equipment she had been coveting. Three yellow stars filled with pinto beans and a yellow half-moon. All four bags were iridescent and glowed in the dark. She had been saving her money to buy them, but every time she had enough, something happened. She had to pay extra lab fees at school herself because there was no money in the house. Her tennis shoes wore out, even when she bought expensive ones. One of her friends' birthdays came up, and she had to buy her a present. She *had* to. They were all so nice to her. But she had vowed to buy the juggling equipment as soon as her cast came off, even if she had to go without lunch for a month.

The angry cat crawled back into its den and went to sleep. Eve could feel it purr inside of her as her stomach settled back into place. She wanted to run over to her father, throw her arms around him, give him a hug, but she couldn't move. There was a tightness in her throat. She knew if she moved, if she acknowledged in any way how she felt, her emotions would come spilling out of her eyes, and she didn't want that. She didn't want him to see her cry. She didn't want anyone to see her cry. She never cried. Never. She had way too much control for that. She had to.

"I thought maybe you could use these when—" He stopped and looked at her, searching her face for some kind of clue. She knew she wondered what she was thinking. She knew he wanted to put his arms around her, but he couldn't do that any more than she could. So they stood facing each other. Father and daughter, each bound by an invisible cord that tied them up and kept them in their own very private, separate worlds.

"How's the arm?" he asked, finally breaking the uneasy silence. "Cast going to come off soon?"

"Yeah," she answered, relieved that the moment of potential contact between them had passed and their normal defenses were hammered back into place. "It itches, but it isn't that bad, only—" She stopped and held her breath. She didn't want to continue.

"Only what?"

"Nothing."

"I know what you were going to say."

"No, you don't," she lied. This was not the time to go into it. She just wanted to get out of there before she changed her mind.

"Thanks for the moon and the stars," she said, taking them from her father's hand and plopping them into the navy canvas bag she always carried with her. Everyone teased her about it. It contained everything she needed—her makeup, an extra change of clothes, money for a cab in case she got stranded somewhere, her schoolbooks, her favorite novels to alleviate the boredom of those long waits for buses and the long bus rides to Delphi's or Binnie and Heather's. They lived on the other side of town. The right side of town where most people had cars. Getting there by bus was a test of ingenuity in itself. She had to transfer twice and walk two miles. At the bottom of the bag were pajamas, an extra toothbrush, toothpaste, and a hairbrush. She traveled around a lot—from friend to friend—when things got heavy at home. In the past few years, she rarely went anyplace without her bag.

She was about to zip it shut when she remembered that she also wanted to take her red oversized sweater, which she had inadvertently left behind. She put her canvas bag down and opened the bottom dresser drawer. When she picked up the sweater, her hand brushed against something hard and cold. Her heart started to pound. She knew what it was without even looking. She kept it in her dresser, tucked away, so she could look at it when she needed to, but she hadn't looked at it much in the past year. Even though she had needed to almost every day. She didn't want to think about her anymore. What good would it do to think about her, anyway? She was gone, and she was never going to come back. Even if she did come back, her father wouldn't let her into the house again. She'd heard him say it a million times. Usually when he was about to pass out. "If she comes wandering up the street, if she comes walking into this house, I swear, I'll throw her right out again. I don't care if she's your mother or not. What kind of woman leaves her family?"

Eve had asked herself the same question often enough, but she didn't want to hear it coming from her father because she always answered the question too.

She always told herself that her mother had run away because her father had kept her a prisoner. Not a real prisoner, of course, but he wouldn't let her do the one thing she wanted more than anything else—to act. And she was talented, too, but she was getting too old to look really good, and she knew that if she didn't give it a go soon, she'd never get her chance. So she left one day while Eve was at school. She left with all her clothes, her jewelry, her makeup, everything she owned. She didn't leave anything behind to remind Eve and her father of her, nothing for them to come upon accidentally and gasp when they remembered her touching it or wearing it. But she was there anyway. All over the house.

For a long time, Eve remembered her every time she walked into the kitchen. She'd come in expecting to see her standing in front of the sink, washing the dishes, or in front of the stove, stirring a pot of soup—proud of her accomplishment. It made Eve smile to remember that. Her mother's creative cooking. She'd open three different kinds of soup and mix them all together, then rave about how wonderful it tasted.

And Eve remembered how her mother looked when she sat in front of her mirror and put her makeup on. She'd suck in her cheeks and brush the blusher on with swift, upward strokes. She drew gray lines on her eyelids, on top and underneath, to accentuate her gray eyes. She concentrated on every little detail till she was satisfied with what she saw in the mirror. Sometimes, she'd just sigh, take it off, and start all over again. Eve couldn't figure out exactly why. She looked beautiful. She always looked beautiful. Even when she didn't wear a touch of makeup. But no one ever saw her without makeup except Eve and her father. Her father thought her mother was beautiful too. He loved to look at her. Eve would see him staring at her across the table. He would look at her while she sat sprawled on the couch watching TV. He bought her jewelry and expensive clothes, even when they couldn't afford it, because the best was never good enough for her mother, never as beautiful as she was.

But after she left, he never wanted to look at her again. Her father tore up all the pictures of her mother, the ones she'd left behind—maybe accidentally, maybe because she thought Eve would want them. Eve was sure her mother had left them for her. She had managed to salvage just this one. She'd bought a frame for it with her own meager allowance and had tucked it into her drawer, away from her father's judgmental eyes.

She put her red sweater back on top of the picture. She'd get it another time. It wasn't that important. She turned to her father and smiled—a little—just to let him know that she wasn't angry with him anymore, but she wasn't going to change her mind about coming back home either. Maybe it would have been better if she had been able to actually tell him she wasn't angry with him. Maybe it would have been better if he had told her exactly why he had been so angry with her when she had come home from Binnie's party and told him that Binnie's stepfather was making a documentary about her and her friends. Maybe. And maybe not. Maybe words weren't necessary. Her father could tell she wasn't angry anymore. Enough time had passed. Two weeks had all but erased the steely spikes of hurt that had been much more painful than the broken arm. And if they weren't exactly erased, at least they were shoved way back there someplace, so far back that they were totally inaccessible to Eve.

And on another level, she blamed herself for her father's anger. She blamed herself for provoking it. On some level, she knew—she had really known all along— how he would react when she told him about the documentary. The same way he reacted when her mother would mention wanting to be in a movie. They didn't need to talk about it. They knew. They simply knew.

She zipped up her canvas bag and sighed. This wasn't going to be as easy as she had thought it would be. In a way, she wished she had been able to hang on to the anger she had felt two weeks ago.

She walked to the front door, wondering if she should give him a quick kiss good-bye. She wanted to, but they weren't a kissing family. At least she and her father weren't. He kissed her mother, she was sure, but never in public, never in front of her. Any display of emotion embarrassed him—when he was sober. When he was drunk, the only emotion he expressed was anger, the pent-up anger he didn't express when he was dry.

"So, bye," she said, opening the door.

"I'll drive you to Delphi's," he offered. "It'll take you forever to get there at this hour—and I don't like you walking around by yourself at night," he added hesitantly, as if he knew he had no right to tell her what he liked and what he didn't like her to do.

"No," she said. "It's okay."

"Call me when you get to Delphi's then," he said softly.

"Yeah," she said, but she didn't turn around to leave yet.

He was staring at her, the same way he used to stare at her mother. He clenched his teeth hard, so hard Eve could almost hear them grind against each other. His jaw tightened as if he were holding in some private terror he couldn't afford to let escape.

"In this light you look just like—" he started to say. Then he stopped himself. "Call me from Delphi's," he said again. "Just to let me know you're all right."

Eve opened the front door and started to walk out.

Without turning around, she asked, "Are you really going to stay dry this time?"

"Really," he whispered, as if he were almost afraid to say it out loud.

"How about popping open a couple of cans of Coke, then?" she said, putting her canvas bag down. "I guess we could try it again. I could stay for a while. See how it works out."

When she turned around to walk back into the room, he was already walking toward the kitchen. She was glad. She didn't want him to see the expression on her face. Her eyes were closed tightly and she was biting her bottom lip.

"By the way," her father said, his voice quavering slightly, "your old juggling balls are on the kitchen counter." He cleared his throat. "I was—ah—tossing them around one night."

She half smiled to herself. She hadn't made any promises or commitments. She could leave anytime, but she'd stay for tonight. She'd stay for awhile, maybe.

He needed her. And after all, how could she abandon him too?

Chapter Two

Eve reached over to turn off her alarm. She was about to suggest they cut morning classes and sleep in when she remembered she was in her own bed, not at Delphi's house. She lay there for a moment, very still, then she curled up into a ball, her arms clasped around her legs, her head tucked down into her chest.

She wanted to stay that way forever. She wasn't ready to go out into the world this morning. Delphi would want details. Binnie and Heather would be concerned about her choice. She hadn't done her homework, and she was so far behind in English she didn't know how she'd ever catch up. Maybe she'd stay home today, do her work, and go back to school tomorrow. She used to do that a lot before she stayed at Delphi's. With her father out of the house by six-thirty, it was no problem. There was no one home to urge her to go to school, and her father was always willing to write an excuse for her when he came home. He never even asked her if she was really sick. All she had to do was indicate in some way that she had stomach cramps, that it was that time of the month, and he would scurry out of the room

11

to get a paper and pen. He'd write the excuse and hand it to her without looking at her.

Even after he lost his job a month ago, he'd be gone by the time she woke up. He'd disappear early every morning looking for work. He'd drive down to the unemployment office and check the bulletin boards for any openings for experienced plumbers. Sometimes he got temporary work. But by the time she had walked out, he was doing odd jobs—painting, carpentry—around people's houses. It depressed him. He was a professional. He took plumbing as seriously as a doctor, lawyer, or teacher would take his or her work. But something had set him off on his last job. He had started drinking more than usual, and when he had a six-pack inside him, he would mumble about his boss, about the way Mr. Johnson treated him. Mr. Johnson didn't respect her father. Of course, Eve knew that her father would never say anything to Mr. Johnson. He'd just smile, nod, and shuffle off. Then he'd think about what Mr. Johnson had said to him all day, and by the time he came home at night, he'd be angry at himself as well as at Mr. Johnson. He'd say to Eve that he was going to tell Johnson to go to hell the next day, then he was going to quit and find himself a decent company to work for.

Eve didn't know if he really would have done that or not. She didn't think he could, but he never got the chance. He started drinking at lunch time instead of just when he came home at night, and that was the one thing Mr. Johnson couldn't tolerate. He canned Judd, and he refused to give him a decent recommendation.

Of course, that just added to her father's frustration, and by that time—the night she broke her arm when he chased her out of the house screaming that no daughter of his was going to be a porno queen—he was pretty much drinking all day.

Porno queen, Eve thought to herself. She wanted to laugh out loud when she thought about it. She didn't know what the hell ever gave him the idea that a documentary had anything to do with pornography. A porno queen! This was the kid who refused to take a shower in gym in front of the other girls even when they teased her unmercifully about it. She was too shy.

She unfurled and stretched out on the bed. Maybe she should go to school and get it over with. She wouldn't be able to study if she stayed home, anyway. She didn't have the self-control. She knew she'd stay in her room and listen to music, or worse, turn on "General Hospital" to see what she had missed in the past month.

When she came out of the bathroom, a strange but pleasant smell assaulted her. She walked into the tiny kitchen, not big enough for a table, just big enough for a counter and three stools. She looked at the third stool for a moment and caught her breath. It happened that way sometimes. A simple thing like three stools for two people would make her throat fill up with a spongy ball so that she couldn't swallow. She coughed, hurling the ball down into her stomach, but an emptiness remained that she couldn't wash away no matter how many times she swallowed.

Her father was standing in front of the stove wearing a huge white apron with "Super Dad" written on it. She had gotten it for him one Father's Day a long time ago, but he had never worn it before.

"Fried eggs," he said, smiling at her. "Just the way you like them."

"Thanks," she said, pleased that her father had gone to all that trouble for her, but she didn't know how she was going to get the eggs down. Her stomach was already in spasm. "They look great, but I don't have time to eat breakfast. I'll miss my bus for school."

"You don't have to take the bus this morning," he said proudly. "I'll drive you to school on my way to work."

"You got a job?" she screamed, excited for him.

"At a new plumbing place in Venice. Fancy place. New equipment. The works. Started three days ago."

"Then why are you still home?" Eve asked, frightened that he would blow this job too.

"We call in at six-thirty every morning, and the secretary tells us where our first appointment is. Mine isn't until eight-thirty—and it's not far from your school, so . . ."

"That's great. That's really great," Eve said, nibbling on the fried eggs.

"Wait!" her father shouted. "There's more."

He opened the oven and took out some hot biscuits. "Ta-da."

"I can't believe it," Eve said, laughing.

"It's a celebration," her father said.

"Yeah," Eve agreed. "It's a celebration."

"They treat you right there," he said as he poured them both hot cups of coffee. "With respect."

"I'm glad," Eve said. "I'm really glad."

She reached over to touch his hand, but he got up to clear the dishes.

"I'll just rinse them off and stack them in the sink while you get your stuff together," he said. "Then we're out of here."

Eve climbed into the battered, old Chevy pickup truck. They had loved it so much when it was new. It had been all shiny. She used to beg to ride in the open backbed with her friends. Her friends loved it too. They'd squeal and laugh and wave to people in cars passing by. They felt special. She felt special. Nobody else's father but hers drove a pickup truck.

As they approached school, Eve started to squirm.
"You can just let me off at the corner," she said.

"Wouldn't think of it," her father said as he pulled
into the parking lot.

"Bye," she yelled, jumping out of the truck as soon
as her father hit the brakes. "See you later."

Eve swung her canvas bag over her shoulder and
headed across the parking lot to the west side of the
building.

Binnie and Heather were just getting out of the used
Toyota their parents had bought them for their sixteenth
birthdays, and Delphi was slipping into her parking
space in her new bright red VW Cabriolet.

Eve was glad to see them, of course. She was always
glad to see her friends. She loved them. She smiled at
Delphi, who couldn't sit still for more than two minutes
at a time, and who was enthusiastic about everything
from heavy-metal music, which the rest of them couldn't
stand, to French, which the rest of them couldn't speak
since they had all opted for Spanish.

Delphi beeped her horn at Eve before she got out of
the car.

"How come you didn't drive to school with Delphi
this morning?" Binnie asked, running up to Eve.

"Stayed at my house last night," Eve said, looking
past Binnie, who was the best all-around female athlete
at school, to her stepsister, Heather, the all-American
beauty. "How's Vince doing?" she asked Heather, who
had gone to the hospital to visit him last night.

"He's a lot better, but he won't be able to run around
much for a while," Heather explained. "I mean, who
could play varsity tennis with four broken ribs?"

"Was he glad you came to see him?" Eve asked,
knowing very well that any guy in the school would
only die to have Heather visit him—especially in a bedroom, even if it was in a hospital. Heather was gor-

geous, and what made her even more beautiful was the fact that she didn't even seem to know it or to care about it. She didn't swing her copper-colored hair for effect, though when she did, it attracted just about everyone's attention. But, Eve knew, Heather swung her hair just to get it out of her eyes.

Binnie and Heather were stepsisters. They had had a falling-out over a guy—the guy who had sent Vince Maggio to the hospital on a stretcher—but they were joined at the hip again, glued together by their mutual horror at what a geek Harris Evans turned out to be.

For a long time Binnie had been Eve's Saturday night date, part of a threesome: Eve, Binnie, and Tony, who played on the boys' varsity baseball team. But lately Binnie and Tony had been spending a lot of time together without her. It wasn't that Eve was jealous. Tony had had a crush on Binnie for years, but, as Binnie used to say, unless Steve Sax suddenly dropped down from the sky and asked her out, she wasn't interested in dating.

Tony wasn't exactly Steve Sax, but Binnie had obviously changed her mind. She had even started to wear skirts occasionally. That was okay with Eve. She had plenty of other things to do with her time, such as practicing juggling.

Delphi, of course, was the most social being in the world and always had parties to go to. Since Eve had been staying at Delphi's, she'd let Delphi coax her into coming along with her most weekends.

The parties were sort of fun, but Eve couldn't stand it when guys came on to her. She liked to dance and fool around, but she didn't like to be maneuvered into dark corners. And she just hated it when some big jerk tried to touch her. She hated being touched. At least she thought she would hate it.

"So, tell us," Delphi squealed. Delphi never just talked. She either squealed, screamed, or whispered if something was really, really important, and in Delphi's life, everything was important.

Eve took out a juggling ball, threw it into the air, and bounced it off her cast. "Tell you what?" she asked innocently, though she knew damn well what Delphi meant.

"What happened last night?"

"Nothing," Eve said, hoping they'd drop the subject. She hated talking about her father. She knew they were all interested because they were her friends, and they loved her, but she also knew that they were curious too. She knew they talked about her father behind her back. They were sympathetic, especially Heather, who thrived on taking care of anyone with a problem. But in spite of their sympathy, Eve knew they were also really getting off on the gossip.

"Eeeeve," Delphi wailed. "Come onnnnn."

Eve rolled her eyes. The kid was tenacious.

"Leave her alone, Delphi," Heather said, giving Delphi a nudge.

"Okay," Delphi said grudgingly. "But are you coming back to my house tonight, or what?"

Before Eve had a chance to answer, Stephanie Brown walked past them and into the side door of the school. Actually, she didn't walk past them, she tripped, dropped all her books, picked them up, and slithered past them as quickly as she could.

"What's wrong with her?" Binnie asked. "She used to be a neat kid. Smart and all. God, she hasn't turned in an English paper all semester. I heard Miss Delgado tell her she'd have to drop out of the honors class if she couldn't get her act together."

"She's all screwed up," Delphi said. "My mom's friends with her mom. The whole family's wacko."

"What do you mean?" Eve asked.

"Nothing," Delphi said. Eve was surprised at her

reluctance to go on. This was the kind of thing that Delphi could hypothesize about for hours.

"I heard her brother's in juvenile," Heather said.

"What!" Binnie said, shocked.

"He's in a detention center."

"I thought only poor kids went there," Eve said.

"You mean because their parents can't afford a good lawyer like my mom to get them off?" Delphi asked.

"I don't know," Eve said, embarrassed by her question. But she had never actually heard of a middle-class kid going to Juvenile, then on to one of the detention centers in the Malibu hills, the ones people euphemistically called "camps." They went to drug rehab centers or to psychiatrists twice a week instead, and all they had to do was report to their probation officers. As far as she knew, rich kids didn't go to jail, unless it was for a major crime. Only kids in her neighborhood went to jail. Stephanie Brown's family lived up the street from Delphi's on a block where every house had its own swimming pool and maid's quarters. The only minority person in that neighborhood, besides household help, was Delphi's mother, who was black.

"So—what's he in for?" Binnie asked as they stood at the bottom of the stairs about to disperse in different directions for their various classes.

Delphi glanced at Eve and shrugged her shoulders. "I forget."

"You do not," Binnie insisted. "What's this big protection scene all of a sudden? You holding out on us 'cause his mother's a friend of your mother's, or what?"

"He has a drinking problem," Delphi said in a rush, as if she wanted to get it over with as quickly as possible. "His mother put him in the hospital to dry out three times in the past year, but he kept sneaking away. He stole her car, drove to Venice, got drunk, and passed out."

"Are you kidding?" Heather asked.

"I'm not kidding," Delphi said. "Mrs. Brown reported her car stolen. That's how they found him."

"And she pressed charges against him?" Binnie asked.

"Yeah," Delphi said. "Keeping him in jail was the only way she knew to keep him alive. She said she'd rather visit him in jail than at the cemetery. He's—he's an alcoholic."

"Well, he could stop," Heather said.

"No, he couldn't," Delphi said, without looking at Eve.

"No wonder Stephanie has problems," Heather said softly.

"I feel sorry for her," Eve said, almost under her breath. She felt more than sorry for Stephanie. She identified with her in a way that none of her friends possibly could.

When she got home from school, Eve finished the breakfast dishes and went into her room. She popped a Bruce Springsteen tape into her tape deck and flopped down on her bed with her navy-blue canvas bag. She unzipped it and took out her books as the phone rang.

"Just wanted to say hi," her father said when she answered.

"Hi," she said. "I just got home."

"I'll see you at six-thirty," he said.

"Okay," she said as she hung up. "Wait," she called into the phone, but it was too late. All she heard was a dial tone. She wanted to ask him if there was anything she could do for dinner. It had been such a long time since she was responsible for meals that she had forgotten all about it. At Delphi's house the housekeeper cooked and put dinner on the table, then she, Delphi, and Delphi's brother cleaned up. At Heather and Binnie's they all took turns cooking unless Binnie's mother got home from the hospital late, or Heather's father was shooting a film, or the girls stayed after school for sports or theater, then they ordered pizza or Chinese food and ate on paper plates.

Eve would miss the commotion around the dinner table. She and her father rarely talked. They were polite. He'd ask her about her day. She'd give him some innocuous details. She'd ask him about his day. He'd say it was fine. Just fine. Then she'd find out what his day was really like later—after he'd had four or five beers. She sighed. It would be nice to have a real family. She almost wished her father would meet someone. Someone lively and talkative, like Delphi's mother. But he never went out with the kind of woman he'd want to introduce to his daughter.

Occasionally, when he was between jobs, Eve would find him passed out in the living room in the morning with some woman he'd picked up in a bar, but by the time she'd get home from school, the woman would be long gone. And besides, somewhere inside, Eve believed that her father was waiting for her mother to come back just as she was, even though he would never admit it in a million years.

Eve got up off of her bed and walked into the living room. She picked up the *TV Guide* to see what was on cable tonight. She wanted to have something to look forward to after she was finished with her homework.

"Wednesday, Wednesday," she said to herself. She went down the listings and stopped at nine o'clock. She should be about finished by then, and even if she wasn't, she'd be too tired to concentrate. *Risky Business*. Terrific. It was only her favorite film. She'd seen it a dozen times, but who cared. Tom Cruise was in it. She'd also seen *Top Gun* and *The Color of Money* three times each.

If Steve Sax was Binnie's fantasy date, Tom Cruise was hers.

The phone rang just as she was about to rush back to her room to do her math assignment.

"You never did tell me what went on at your house last night," Delphi said.

"You're never going to guess what's on cable tonight," Eve screamed.

"*Risky Business*, nine o'clock," Delphi said, bored.

"How'd you know?"

"English may not be my best subject, but I can read," Delphi said.

"You want to know what my fantasy is?" Eve asked.

"Sure."

Eve giggled, something she rarely ever did. "My fantasy is—promise you won't laugh?"

"No," Delphi said.

"Okay. I'll tell you anyway. My fantasy is that I'll have a date with Tom Cruise for my seventeenth birthday."

"Oh sure, go for the absolutely unattainable," Delphi said. "Why don't you fantasize about someone available once in a while? You've never even had a date with anyone, pea brain, and it's not 'cause they haven't asked you, either."

Eve and Delphi went over the math homework on the phone, then Eve took a short bathroom break before starting her social studies. It was true, she didn't go out with guys, but there was nothing wrong with her, she decided. They just didn't live up to her standards, and she wasn't willing to settle for less. So she speculated that unless Tom Cruise suddenly materialized, it looked as if she was going to remain dateless for a hell of a long time.

When she got back into her room, the phone rang again.

"Damn, I'm never going to get finished in time," she said as she picked it up.

"My mom did some legal work for Disney," Delphi said without taking a breath. "She said she'd try to get you an introduction to the man of your dreams. But only an introduction, since he just got married."

Eve's stomach flipped upside-down, and she broke out into a sweat; then she let out a scream. An introduction was good enough for her. "Oh my God. Are you kidding?"

"Hey, I wouldn't kid about a serious thing like that, would I?"

By the time seven o'clock rolled around, Eve was a wreck. For two reasons. One, she couldn't stop thinking about Delphi's phone call, and two, her father wasn't home yet.

When she heard his truck pull up at seven-thirty, she froze. She listened for the door to slam before getting up from her bed. It slammed, and her father came into the house singing. Eve stiffened and held her breath. He was drunk. She was sure he was drunk. She didn't move.

"Sorry I'm late," he called from the kitchen. "I have a surprise."

I'll bet you do, she thought. But it was really no surprise after all. She hadn't expected him to stay sober, had she?

Wearily, she got up from her bed and made her way into the kitchen. There on the counter was a beautiful bunch of carnations and roses and on two plates was her favorite dinner, linguine with clam sauce.

"Sorry I'm so late," her father apologized. "I'm telling you, I waited forty-five minutes in Colombo's for this pasta. Hope you're not mad at me."

"I'm not mad at you," Eve said, smelling the flowers. Without lifting her face, she added, "I'm happy. Really, really happy."

"What are we waiting for, then?" her father asked cheerfully. "Let's dig in."

Chapter Three

Eve and Binnie drove along the coast and into Marina Del Rey. The weather was exceptionally warm for January, probably because the Santa Anas had blown in from the east. Eve could always tell when the Santa Ana winds blew west. Her nose would run and she sneezed nonstop.

"Let's go to that new fifties restaurant in the Marina," Binnie suggested. "Heather was there with Vince last week."

"Vince?" Eve asked, raising her eyebrows.

"He's out of the hospital, but he still can't drive. She took him to his doctor, and they stopped there afterward."

"Okay," Eve said. "Sounds good to me."

They pulled into the parking lot and walked toward the brightly lit restaurant.

"Cool," Binnie said. "Look at those light fixtures."

"Think they're really from the fifties?" Eve asked.

"Nah, they're probably new, but they're really good reproductions of the originals."

They sat down in a booth with a gray Formica table

and huge gray leather seats. "Sha-boom, sha-boom, ya-dadadadada, sha-boom, sha-boom—" rang out on the jukebox, and both the girls laughed.

"I love it," Eve said. "Let's see what else they have."

"Let's order first," Binnie said, looking at the largest menu she'd ever seen.

After the waitress took their order, Binnie and Eve studied the chrome jukebox sitting next to their table. For twenty-five cents, they could relive those golden days of the fifties their parents were so fond of talking about.

"Little Richard. I love Little Richard," Binnie said. "Got a quarter?"

Eve dug into her purse and pulled out a quarter. "Here, you play a Little Richard song, and play Johnny Ray for me."

"Who's he?"

" 'If your sweetheart sends a letter of good-bye,' " Eve wailed, imitating Johnny Ray.

"Yuk, I hate sad songs," Binnie said, cutting her off.

"Then you pick something for me," Eve said.

"I'm going to the bathroom," Binnie said, getting up from the table. "Want to come?"

"Nah, I'll wait here."

"Then you pick another song."

Eve pushed the button on the jukebox for the Everly Brothers' "Wake Up Little Suzy" as Binnie slipped away from the table.

Eve juggled the silverware as the music played, bouncing it off her cast. Binnie took her good old time getting back, and Eve was worried that her hamburger would be cold, but when Binnie finally returned, she didn't even look at her food. She was so excited she could hardly talk.

"He's here," she stammered.

"Who?" Eve asked

"Shush, not so loud," Binnie warned.

"Who's here?" Eve whispered.

"Him."

"Binnie, you're not making any sense," Eve said.

"Don't look now," Binnie warned, "but right in back of us about two tables down, sitting with his back to you is—you're not going to believe this—I swear—"

Eve started to turn around to see who Binnie was talking about.

"Don't turn around," Binnie hissed. "Be cool. For God's sake, be cool."

"Well, tell me who it is, then," Eve said, annoyed with the childish way Binnie was behaving.

"Tom Cruise."

Eve's mouth dropped open, and her eyes formed huge, round saucers in her head. "Serious?" she asked expectantly.

"Serious," Binnie said, leaning in toward her.

Eve started to turn around again.

"No. No. You'll spoil everything if you stare at him."

"How can I stare at him if his back's toward me?" Eve asked. "I just want to get a quick look."

"He'll know you're staring," Binnie said. "He'll sense it. Movie stars always do."

"How do you know?"

"I know. I know. Just take my word for it. We've got to figure out what to do."

"I can't think straight," Eve said. "I can't breathe."

"Okay. Just stay cool."

"How can I stay cool? I'm already totally out of control."

"Okay. Okay. Here's what you do. Just get up casually and walk to the bathroom. I mean, that's natural. Right?"

"Yeah, it's natural, except that I can't walk. My knees have turned to jelly."

"Look, go to the john, but don't even look in his direction. You'll only be able to see him from the back on your way there, anyway. Stay in the john for a few minutes, then come out, real casually, and walk past his table. Maybe you can slip or something. Lose your balance. Then he'll have to give you a hand, and you'll get to meet him."

"I can't," Eve whispered.

"Why?"

"I'm too nervous."

"Don't be silly. He's just a person. I mean what's he going to do, break your arm or something?" Binnie said without even thinking.

Eve's eyes opened even wider.

"Sorry. I didn't mean that. I'm sorry. Really," Binnie said, wishing she could take her words back.

"I know. I know."

"Okay. I got a better idea. We'll ask the waitress to take a note over to him."

"I don't know," Eve said.

"Yeah, come on. Write it."

"I don't have a piece of paper."

"I'll get one for you," Binnie volunteered.

"No," Eve shouted. "Then you'll have to leave the table, and I'll be sitting here all by myself. What if he walks past? I'll die."

"Just go up to him and tell the truth, then," Binnie suggested. "Tell him you're his biggest fan ever. That you've seen all his movies eighty times—"

"Not eighty—"

"What's the difference? Just tell him you want to meet him. Tell him you love him."

"Are you crazy?" Eve asked.

"Yeah. Sometimes." Binnie laughed.

"I know," Eve said. "Let's call Delphi. She'll know what to do."

"Fine. Get up from the table and go call her."

"I can't," Eve admitted.

"I'll call her." Binnie got up before Eve could stop her.

Eve bit her nails as she watched Binnie walk over to the phone booth and put a quarter in. She held her breath as she waited for the word, but a few seconds later Binnie turned around, shook her head no, and mouthed the words, "She's not home."

Eve was disappointed. She had to think of something fast. What if he left and she missed her chance?

Binnie was walking toward her, but she didn't stop at the table. She kept right on walking, past Eve, right over to Tom Cruise's table. Eve was sure that was where she was going. She wanted to die on the spot.

"You're Tom Cruise, right?" she heard Binnie say.

Eve was so embarrassed she buried her head in her hands.

"No," she heard. "I'm not Tom Cruise."

"Listen, I know you are," Binnie insisted. "But I don't blame you for pretending you're not."

"I'm not," the male voice said. "My name's Torbin Black."

"That's a good one, but a little too theatrical," Binnie said. "You should have picked something more normal like Eric Feldman."

Eve heard Tom laugh. "I didn't pick it," he said. "My mother did."

"Okay, listen," Binnie said. "Your biggest fan is sitting at a table right behind you. I mean it. She's seen all your movies a dozen times. Well, maybe not a dozen, but who's counting? She's too shy to come over and introduce herself to you, but you've just got to meet her. Please. I mean, will it hurt you?"

"You're very persistent," Tom said.

"Anything for a friend," Binnie said.

"Look, I'd love to meet Tom Cruise's biggest fan, but I'm not Tom Cruise."

"Okay, tell you what—just come over and meet her. I'll introduce you any way you want. Deal?"

"Deal."

"So what did you say I should call you?"

Eve heard Tom laugh again. God, he was wonderful.

"Just call me Torbin," he said. "I'll feel more comfortable that way."

Binnie giggled as she led Tom over to the table. Eve was so embarrassed she could barely look at him. This was her big moment, and she was totally blowing it. Totally.

"I'm sorry Binnie dragged you over here," she said finally. "I know you must have better things to do."

"Not really," Tom said, smiling at her.

I can't believe this, Eve thought.

"I'm glad Binnie dragged me over here. I didn't realize Tom Cruise's biggest fan would be so—nice," he said, almost blushing.

Eve was really touched. He was shy. He was really shy. Just as she was.

"I really do think you're a wonderful actor," Eve said, sneaking a good look at him.

"I think I'm a good actor too," Tom said, "but unless you've seen me in something at UCLA, I don't understand how you'd know that."

"Just go along with him," Binnie whispered.

Eve started to laugh nervously. She wasn't sure how she was supposed to act.

"Listen, Eve's going to be seventeen in two weeks," Binnie said.

"Binnie!" Eve warned.

"I was just going to say that you wanted to meet him before your seventeenth birthday," Binnie explained.

"Sure," Eve said, under her breath.

"Happy birthday," Tom said.

Quick, Eve said to herself. Think of something sophisticated to say, or he'll leave.

"My friend's mother is a lawyer at Disney," Eve said.

"That's nice," Tom said, looking at her a little strangely.

"She's worked with your manager. You know, on the contracts for *The Color of Money.*"

"Well, you'll have to introduce us sometime."

"You and my friend's mother?"

"No, me and my so-called manager."

They all started to laugh. This was a crazy game, but if that was the way he wanted to play it, it was all right with Eve. She just couldn't believe he was standing there talking to her.

"Would you like to sit down?" she asked him, surprised she had so much nerve.

"Love to," he said, "but I have to run. Sorry."

"I understand," Eve said, disappointed.

"I really would like to stay, though," he said, looking straight into Eve's eyes.

That was the nicest lie she'd ever heard. She almost melted into the table along with her hot fudge sundae, which had also turned to mush.

He started to walk away, then he turned back to them. "See those light fixtures?" he asked.

"Yeah," they both said.

"They look just like fixtures from the fifties, don't they?"

"Exactly," Eve said.

"But they're not," he said. "They're reproductions."

"Yeah, that's what we thought," Binnie said.

"Most people can't tell the difference," he said. "But there is a difference, even if they look alike. And you know what? Sometimes the reproductions are an even better quality than the real thing."

He winked at Eve and Binnie and took off.

"I can't believe it. I just can't believe it," Eve said.

"Believe it." Binnie laughed.

"It was almost a date," Eve said.

"It wasn't a date," Binnie said, "and almost doesn't count. You should have given him your phone number."

"I couldn't do that."

"I could have, but you obviously didn't want to me interfere."

"I would have been mortified," Eve said, pushing the melted ice cream around in the glass dish.

"Yeah, but you might have had a date on your seventeenth birthday."

"He is really cute, though, isn't he?"

"He's cute."

"I mean really cute. Really, really cute."

"He's cute."

"He's unbelievable. Much cuter in person than he is in his movies."

Chapter Four

Eve stood in front of the living room window watching for Delphi's red Cabriolet to cruise down the street and screech to a stop in front of her house. She was excited. Today was her seventeenth birthday, and even though her big wish was obviously not going to come true, she was going to have a terrific day. Delphi, Binnie, Heather, and she were heading for the Venice board-walk to spend the day and then meet her father at her favorite restaurant. He was treating them all to dinner. That was the present she had asked for.

Eve checked her watch. It was already noon. By the time they got there and parked, it would be one o'clock. Everything would be crowded, and the boardwalk would be packed by then because it was the first sunny day in a week. Californians feel cheated if it rains more than three days in a row, and on the first sunny day after a week of rain, nobody stays in the house.

Delphi started honking her horn while she was still a block away. Eve recognized the code, one long beep and two short ones. She ran out of the house, yelling good-bye to her father, who was in the kitchen fixing lunch and listening to an opera on the radio. She smiled. Things had really changed, after all. For the better. Gradually her father was returning to that distant memory she had of him from when she was a little kid. She hadn't heard him play opera for years, but as she listened to it now, she remembered his singing along when she was two or three. He had a loud, booming voice. He was humming along with "*La donna è mobile*" now. Maybe someday he'd feel like blasting it out again. He used to sing, then laugh, pick her up, twirl her around in the air, and say, "*La donna è mobile*—woman is fickle—oh yes, she is," and Eve would giggle and say, "Fickle, pickle, tickle," and her father would put her down and tickle her.

She wasn't imagining it. He used to tickle her—and put his arms around her—and hug her. She knew he had.

As she got into the car, everyone screamed, "Happy birthday!" She could barely hear it above the music on Delphi's state-of-the-art stereo, which blasted from speakers in the front and back and from the two front doors too.

" 'Like a monkey on your back, ya need it. But do you love it enough to leave it?' " they all sang with Phil Collins as the car rolled along the ocean to Venice.

They drove around for twenty minutes trying to find a free parking space. As usual, Venice was so parked up, people were leaving their cars in red zones and towaway areas, hoping the police would be too busy with other things to ticket them.

"Okay, this is enough," Delphi said. "If we all pitch in, it'll only cost us fifty cents apiece to park in a lot."

"Let's go for it," Binnie said. "Though it really annoys me to pay for parking."

"Me, too," Delphi said, "but it's Eve's birthday, so let's make an exception."

They pulled into a lot right in the middle of all the action and wandered over to a group of people who were gathering around a black comedian.

"I've heard him before," Binnie said. "He's better than Eddie Murphy."

"He looks a little like Eddie Murphy," Heather said.

"A little," Binnie agreed. "Let's stay and watch."

"Okay. Okay," the comedian said, leaning toward the crowd conspiratorially. "We're going to use a little psychology here. See all those dudes walking past? Well, we're going to get them to stop and catch my show. I say 'we' 'cause you all are going to help me. Now when I raise my hand, I want you to clap and shout as loud as you can."

Everybody laughed good-naturedly.

"Okay. Now," the comedian said, raising his hand.

The audience laughed some more, but everybody did what he had asked them to do. They clapped and shouted.

"Louder. Louder," he mouthed, and the crowd yelled even louder. Eve and her friends were jumping up and down, shouting.

Pretty soon the entire area around the comedian was four or five deep with people who had gathered around to see what was going on. And he was so good nobody left.

"Come here. Come on," he said, pointing to Eve.

Eve looked around. Was he talking to her?

"Yeah, you. I'm talking to you," he said.

Eve giggled.

"Come on over here. I won't bite."

Binnie and Delphi gave her a shove forward, but she took two steps back. She didn't mind juggling in front of a crowd, but she wasn't sure what this guy was going to do.

"Come on, trust me," he said winking at her.

What the hell, she thought, laughing as she stepped out of the crowd to the center of the circle where he was standing.

Everyone clapped.

"You see this young lady here—what's your name, young lady?"

"Eve."

"Eve—huh, well, I'd sure like to take a bite of your apple, Eve."

Eve blushed.

"Oh boy," he said, slapping himself on the face, "sometimes I just can't control my mouth."

Everyone laughed, but Eve relaxed. They weren't laughing at her expense. They were in a good mood, and the guy was really funny.

"You know," he continued, "I bet you think, What is that colored guy going to say next? Right? Well, I'm going to ask Eve to be my assistant while I show you a little something. Remember way back about a minute ago when I was so naughty and told this beautiful, blond, young lady that I'd like to take a bite out of her apple?"

Everyone shouted, "Yes."

"Well, she turned bright red, didn't she?"

He waited for everyone to respond, then he went on. "And if she gets up in the morning, and it's colder than a witch's—" He paused. Everyone started to giggle. "No. No. I'm not going to say what you think I am. And it's colder than a witch's frozen pizza, Eve here turns blue. Right?"

Everyone yelled, "Right," again.

"And if I run up behind her and scare the sh—" He stopped, looked around, then took his baseball cap off and slapped the side of his leg with it. "I know what you thought I was going to say. You thought I was going to use profanity, didn't you? Wrong! I was going to say,

'If I run up behind her and scare the shoes off of her—' "
He laughed, and so did the audience. "If I scare the
shoes off of her, she'll turn even whiter than she already
is. Now, look at me. If I'm embarrassed, I'm black. If
I'm cold, I'm black. If I get the shoes scared off me,
I'm still black. Black. Black. Black. And you people
call *us* colored!"

"He's wonderful," Eve said as they all held up dollar
bills, which he picked up with a long rod with pincers.
Legally, he wasn't allowed to ask for money and put
his hand out to receive it, but hell, he wasn't touching
it, he said, so hold up those paper bills. There was also
a hat on the ground for coins.

"Let's walk down to the pier and catch the chain saw
juggler," Heather suggested.

"Let's stop and get some frozen yogurt first," Binnie
said as she headed across the boardwalk. Various food
stands hung out of dilapidated buildings like overripe
tomatoes on a vine left unattended for too long. Some
were more appetizing than others, but the smells of
pizza, sausages, burgers, and fries mingled in the air as
soon as they crossed from the beach side of the narrow
walkway to the buildings. Scuzzy-looking vendors in
white T-shirts, spattered with grease, leaned out of their
open windows and called for the next order.

They stopped at a spotless yogurt store and bought
frozen yogurt. Then they walked slowly toward the pier,
weaving in and out of the skaters and skateboards, the
young couples and older people all mixed together. Even
a couple of L.A. cops came by on roller skates. They
looked at the two men and a woman dressed in white
who stood in front of three stools giving people shiatsu
massages for five bucks apiece.

"Exhibitionists," Delphi said, disgusted.

"No difference between that and chain saw juggling,"
Heather said.

"Everybody likes attention," Binnie said as they walked past.

When they got to the chain saw juggler, he was just about to do his main trick, the finale of his act, a combination juggling act and comedy routine. He picked up a chain saw and turned it on. The buzz always made Eve queasy. It sped through her stomach. She stepped back, almost afraid of the noise, but she was as fascinated as ever by the trick. This guy was the ultimate juggler. Who wouldn't be fascinated? Especially her. She patted her new juggling equipment, which was in her purse. She had left her big canvas bag at home today for the first time in two years.

"Everybody step back," he warned as he turned off the saw for a moment. "We don't want any accidents here. And, of course, if anything does happen, don't forget to call an ambulance, 'cause I'm outta here."

He turned the chain saw on again, threw it up in the air while the audience gasped, and caught it by the handle. Then he threw it even higher. The audience applauded. Eve knew he had to be absolutely sure of himself to perform a trick like that. She wondered how long he had practiced it and how, in fact, he had practiced it without losing a finger or a toe. She wondered if she'd ever be as sure about herself as he was about performing that trick.

They watched the show again from the beginning, then they wandered off, stopping to poke into stores or admire the garishly bright new Venice Beach T-shirts piled on wooden tables in front of stores to catch the tourists' eyes. After all, where can you buy two T-shirts for five dollars, or earrings for a dollar? Of course, the last time Eve had bought earrings at the beach, her ears had gotten infected, and she had to go to a doctor. The pretty pink and white shells she had bought for a buck had wound up costing her thirty-five. She could have bought a pair of gold ones for that price.

"God, what is going on here?" Heather asked, looking around.

"What do you mean?" Binnie asked.

"The people," Heather said, frowning.

"There's always weird people here," Delphi said. "Even if they're straight during the week, this is a place to be weird on weekends."

"That's not what I meant," Heather said. "Look at all the people panhandling today, and walking around in a daze, and stuff. I can't stand it. It's so pitiful."

"It's not your problem," Delphi said. "The police usually keep them under control on weekends, but there do seem to be more bums than usual today. It's really disgusting."

"It's not disgusting," Heather said. "It's sad. Really, really sad."

"Like I said, it's not your problem."

"Then whose is it?" Heather asked.

"Come on, Heather, it's Eve's birthday. Just leave it alone today, will you?"

"It's just—"

"Just nothing. They're always here. They always have been, and always will be. You just noticed them today, that's all," Delphi said, annoyed.

"You're right," Eve said. "I'm usually so busy looking at the shops and the entertainers and the weirdness that I never noticed all the—" She stopped. "All the drunks," she said quietly.

"Hey, lots of things aren't what they seem to be at first," Delphi said. "That's life."

"I guess," Eve mumbled.

"Hey," Delphi yelled suddenly, dragging Eve by the sleeve of her jacket. "You gotta come into this store. You're going to love it. I promise."

"I don't really feel like shopping," Eve said. The fun had dropped out of her day and had dripped to the ground like the sad remains of an ice cream cone.

"Well, I do," Delphi said, pulling her along and giving Heather a dirty look at the same time.

"Come on, Eve," Heather said, brightening up. "This store is unbelievable."

Eve let herself be dragged into the little shop with hand-painted and tie-dyed sweats. They were happy clothes. Some of the sweatshirts had Kabuki actors painted on them, their stark white makeup lighting up the black shirts. Some of them had Greek theater masks, the laughing masks and the frowning ones.

Eve looked around. There were more clothes packed into this tiny space than she had ever seen, and a woman was sitting behind a counter painting more sweatshirts and jackets.

She walked over to watch the woman. The woman smiled at her. She was painting a picture of Bruce Springsteen on a jeans jacket. She turned the jacket over and showed it to Eve. Springsteen memorabilia had already been painted all over it. Lines of his music. Springsteen in front of a microphone with his red bandanna around his head. Springsteen's famous rear end with a bandanna sticking out of his jeans' pocket. Eve was awed.

"That is so fabulous," she said to the woman.

"This is my specialty," the woman said.

"I love it."

"It's for sale."

"I could never afford it," Eve said wistfully.

"It's not that much," the woman said.

"Anything over five dollars is too much for me," Eve said, laughing. "Not that it isn't worth a lot of money. It is, and I'd buy it in a minute if I could."

"It's Eve's birthday," Delphi said, walking up behind Eve.

"Well, in that case," the woman said, "we'll have to give her a present."

Eve was too embarrassed to speak. She nudged Delphi.

"If you just wait for one minute until this dries," the woman said, "it's yours."

"What?" Eve asked. She was sure she had heard wrong.

"It's yours," the woman said. "Your birthday present."

She took out a hair dryer and started to blow hot air on the piece she had just finished. Eve couldn't take her eyes off the jacket. She absolutely coveted it, but she thought the woman was teasing her.

She heard Delphi, Binnie, and Heather all laugh behind her. They knew it was a joke, but she couldn't move anyway.

The woman finished and held the jacket out to Eve. "Try it on."

Eve took it from her in a daze and put it on. It was fabulous.

"Happy birthday, Eve," the woman said. "Hope you like it."

"But I can't—" Eve started to say.

"Yes, you can," the woman said. "It's already been taken care of."

"What do you mean?" Eve asked.

"It's been paid for."

"This is the best birthday I've ever had," Eve said, beaming at her jacket.

"Swear?" Delphi said.

"Swear," Eve said as they walked out of the store.

"Listen, dork, don't you want to know who bought it for you?" Binnie asked.

Eve looked at her, confused. She thought Delphi, Heather, and Binnie had pitched in to buy it for her.

"The owner's nice, and all, but she's not in business because she gives away hundred-dollar jackets to birthday girls," Binnie said, laughing. "And we *are* your best friends, but—"

"Your father ordered it for you," Delphi said. "He fixed Sara's plumbing a few weeks ago, and she was working on a jacket like this one when he was at her house."

"My father?" Eve asked. Her father couldn't afford a present this extravagant, but she was absolutely thrilled with it. She couldn't wait to meet him at Yanks and tell him how much she loved him.

"Quick—back into the store," Delphi said as they were walking away.

"Why?" Eve asked.

"Just go in before she sees us," Delphi said. "We don't want to deal with Stephanie Brown today."

But they didn't have to worry about dealing with Stephanie. Stephanie didn't even see them, though they hadn't gone back into the store. She had walked right past them, looking through them, her eyes glazed, her hair matted and dirty, her clothes torn and covered with mud.

"She wasn't in school Friday," Binnie said.

"What happened to—" Heather started to say.

"Come on," Delphi said. "It's late. We promised to meet Eve's dad at Yanks at six."

They turned around and walked to Delphi's car, but Eve couldn't shake the picture of Stephanie from her mind.

When they pulled up in front of Yanks it was only five-thirty, so they decided to park and walk around, looking into the store windows on Beverly Drive. They didn't get into Beverly Hills much, and these shops had clothes they never saw in Belmont.

They parked two blocks from the restaurant, in the first spot they could find, and worked their way up and down the street, stopping in front of every shop. It wasn't quite Rodeo Drive, but it was close. Not even Delphi shopped here, though her mother did.

"Oh, no," Delphi suddenly shouted. "Look what time it is. We're fifteen minutes late."

"How'd that happen?" Binnie asked.

"I don't know, but we better run," Eve said as they took off down the street.

It was twenty after six by the time they reached the restaurant. Eve was sure her father would be waiting inside, so they went right in.

"Do you have a reservation?" the hostess asked.

"Yes," Eve said. "The name is Morrison."

"I see your name here," the hostess said. "Your table's ready. Is all of your party here?"

"I think my father's inside," Eve said.

"Not yet," the hostess said.

"Maybe he walked up the street to look for us," Eve said. "You guys stay here. I'll go take a look."

Eve ran out of the restaurant just as her father was coming out of the bar next door.

She froze.

"There you are," he said, smiling at her.

She just stared at him, unable to say a word.

He looked at her for a moment before he understood. "The phone's out of order in Yanks," he said. "I used the phone next door to call home, see if there was some change in plans or something. I got worried when you were late."

Eve wanted to believe him. She wanted desperately to believe him, but she didn't, and she didn't want to get close enough to him to find out if her suspicions were justified. She didn't want to smell his Clorets breath, which wouldn't quite hide the odor of booze.

"Delphi, Binnie, and Heather are waiting inside," she said finally.

"Did you have fun?" he asked.

"Lots," she said. "Thanks for the jacket. I love it," she whispered, but her tone was dry, and her voice cracked, so it sounded as though she didn't really mean it.

After they were seated, she excused herself and headed for the women's room. She wanted to be alone for a moment, to gather herself together.

She knew her father had been hurt by the way she had acted. She had planned to throw her arms around him and thank him for the most wonderful present she had ever received, but when she saw him coming out of the bar, she couldn't. And he knew it. She couldn't trust him. And he knew that too.

She sighed as she walked to the back of the restaurant. Outside the rest rooms was a pay phone with a big sign on it: OUT OF ORDER.

Chapter Five

"Eve. Eve," Binnie shouted as she raced out of the theater building.

"What?" Eve asked in a panic.

"I went into the theater to find Heather so I could get the car key," Binnie explained, "and—"

"Is Heather all right?" Eve asked, concerned.

"She's fine," Binnie said impatiently. "Eve—" Binnie grabbed hold of her. "He's in there."

"Who?" Eve asked.

"Torbin Black."

"Who is Torbin Black?" Eve asked.

"Torbin Black!"

"I heard you the first time," Eve said.

"The guy from Edy's."

"Edy's?"

"Why are you being so dense?" Binnie shouted.

"Why are you acting so crazy?" Eve asked.

"Edy's—the fifties restaurant in the Marina."

"Torbin Black!" Eve shouted. Then she put her hand over her mouth. How could one person be so uncool? "What is Tom Cruise doing here?"

"Eve," Binnie said seriously. "You are not going to believe this."

"Probably not," Eve said.

"His name *is* Torbin Black."

"You mean that's Tom Cruise's real name?"

"Eve—I mean that's *his* real name."

"You mean he's not Tom Cruise?"

"He's not Tom Cruise."

"But he looks more like Tom Cruise than Tom Cruise does."

"He's not Tom Cruise. I promise."

"Serious?"

"Serious. Miss Raden said so."

"What did she say?"

"I went in there looking for Heather, and I see this guy, and I recognize him right away, of course, and I almost flip out. I'm standing there, just staring at him with my tongue hanging out, and he comes over to me just like that, and says, 'Hi.' "

"He just comes over and says hi? Just like that?"

"Yeah. Only I'm too freaked out to even say anything, so he says, 'I guess you don't remember me. I met you about a month ago at Edy's in the Marina.' "

"He remembered you?"

"Yeah."

"And?"

"And Lisa Raden comes up at that point and asks how we know each other. He tells her. Then she tells me that he's doing an internship for this technical theater course he's taking at UCLA, and he's going to be helping her out with the new play."

"Come on," Eve said. "Don't be so naive. It's Tom Cruise. He's probably doing some research for some movie he's doing about high school or something."

"No. No. That's what I said too. I mean after he walked away. But Raden just laughed and said she wished that were true. It would be great publicity for the department.''

''His name's really Torbin Black? He's not Tom Cruise?''

''That's what I've been trying to tell you for ten minutes.''

''What a disappointment.''

''Well, he looks like Tom Cruise.''

''Yeah, but it's not the same thing.''

''So what? Maybe this version is better. Remember what he said about the light fixtures?''

''No, I don't remember what he said about the light fixtures,'' Eve said. ''And who cares, anyway?''

''You should meet him.''

''I did meet him.''

''I mean, you should really meet him.''

''I don't want to really meet him. I have better things to do,'' Eve said.

''Like what?''

''Like going to the doctor. I'm getting my cast off this afternoon.''

''Just meet him. I'll drive you to your doctor's appointment.''

''Why do you want me to meet him so badly?'' Eve asked. ''You have a stake in this or something?''

''Or something,'' Binnie said, laughing.

''Okay,'' Eve said, laughing too. ''But it isn't going to do any good. I'm waiting for the real thing.''

''Just meet him,'' Binnie said. ''You don't have to marry him.''

Binnie all but pushed Eve into the theater. Eve looked around, but she didn't see Torbin. She was about to walk back out again when someone came up from behind her and handed her a book.

''You'd be perfect for Carol,'' he said.

She turned around. It was Torbin.

"I'm not auditioning," she said. "I just came in to—"

He smiled at her, and his eyes crinkled at the corners. A dimple spread down his left cheek, and his straight white teeth almost knocked her out with their brightness. He had chocolate-colored eyes. Not brown. Chocolate.

"You should audition," he insisted.

"I'm not in the theater department," she explained.

"Lisa Raden said the auditions were open. You don't have to be in the theater department."

"I can't act."

"Have you ever tried?"

"Not really."

"You have presence," he said.

"Presence?"

"Electricity," he whispered. "You would draw people to you if you were on stage." He chuckled. "You draw people to you even when you're not on stage."

What a line, she thought. But somehow she felt herself getting hooked on it.

"My cast," she said, holding up her arm.

"Might be a problem," he said. "When's it coming off?"

"This afternoon," Binnie said, answering for her.

"That solves that," he said, laughing.

"There are other problems." She looked at Binnie for support, but Binnie wasn't going to support her reticence.

"Just give it a try," he said. "What have you got to lose?"

"Plenty," Eve said, trying to hand him back the script.

"I'll ask Lisa if you can go first," he said, obviously refusing to take no for an answer.

"All right. I'll read for the dumb part," she said, laughing, "but I'll probably look like a clown."

"If you do, we'll use you during the intermission to entertain the audience," he said.

"She juggles too," Binnie added.

"Ohhhh, a woman of many talents, I see," he said, laughing. "Wait here for a minute. I'll see when the auditions are going to start and if you can go first."

"All right," Eve promised. "I'll wait."

"Aw right!" Binnie yelled.

"You're such a jerk," Eve said. "Why'd you get me into this?"

"I didn't get you into anything," Binnie said innocently.

"Why'd I get me into it, then?" Eve said. "I haven't even read *Lemon Sky*. I don't know anything about this play."

"Then you probably don't have anything to worry about, do you?" Binnie asked.

"Well, I don't want to make a fool out of myself," Eve said.

"What do you care?" Binnie asked. "You're not in the drama department. They don't expect you to do a good job."

"Yeah, but—"

"Yeah, but what?"

"You know."

"No, I don't," Binnie said.

"He's cute."

"Yeah, but he's not Tom Cruise," Binnie teased.

"I know," Eve said defensively.

"Okay," Torbin said, running back to them. "Lisa said you could audition first since you have to get to the doctor. Have you had a chance to look over the script?"

"No," Eve said. "Maybe I should come back tomorrow."

"Eve Morrison," Miss Raden called. "Let's see you up on stage."

Eve froze.

"Break a leg," Torbin said.

"Very funny," Eve said. "You mean as long as I'm going to the doctor, anyway—"

The three of them started to laugh as Eve jumped up onto the stage.

"I know this is a cold reading," Miss Raden said. "So I'm not expecting perfection today. This will give me a chance to see what's out there and to decide who will come back tomorrow for callbacks. Callbacks will be posted on the bulletin board outside the main entrance to the theater. We'll go over the characters more carefully tomorrow and determine just which character each of you will be auditioning for. Right now, you're just auditioning, period. So relax."

Oh sure, relax, Eve thought. Come on, the voice inside her said. This isn't any different from juggling in front of a group.

Yeah, but when I juggle, I don't have to talk, she said to herself.

They're not *your* words, the voice said. What do you care?

That's true, she thought. Let Lanford Wilson take the blame. He wrote the damn play.

"Okay," Miss Raden said. "Let's try Carol's speech on page forty-one."

Eve flipped to page forty-one and looked over the speech briefly. It wasn't too bad. But that didn't stop her from being incredibly nervous. The sweat under her arms was quickly rolling its way to the waistline of her jeans, where it gathered in two soggy puddles. Yuk, it was so uncomfortable.

She cleared her throat, but nothing came out of her mouth when she tried to speak.

"May I start again?" she asked. Then she realized how stupid that was. She hadn't started in the first place.

"Take your time," Miss Raden said.

Somehow she got out the first two lines of the speech without collapsing onto the stage or throwing up all over Miss Raden, who was sitting in the first row. She didn't know where Torbin had gone.

I'm this far into it, I might as well continue, she thought. At least nobody's walking out.

"Good," Miss Raden said in a rather noncommittal tone when she finished the last line.

Eve looked down at her for some encouragement, but Miss Raden was already calling Joy Ferguson's name, and Joy bounded up to the stage, almost knocking Eve over, so Eve gave up the area and walked to the back of the auditorium where Binnie was waiting for her.

"That was really lousy, huh?" she asked.

"Well, it wasn't Meryl Streep," Binnie said. "But you have nothing to be ashamed of."

"Thanks for the compliment," Eve said sarcastically. "I'll do the same for you someday."

"You weren't auditioning for the Royal Vic." Binnie laughed. "This is a high school play. Come on. Let's split."

When Eve got back from the doctor's, she went into her room and lay down on her bed. She felt really strange. In the first place, out of her cast, her arm felt like a wounded dove. It just kind of lay there beside her, the muscles gone limp with disuse. It was as if she had forgotten how to lift it. She knew that muscles atrophied when they weren't used. It had been two months since she had used her arm, and it was painful to lift it now.

In the second place, there was the problem of the play. What if she did get a part? What would she do about that? How had she let herself get talked into it? Easy, the voice said. You wanted to be talked into it. You've wanted to be in a play for years, but you never had the nerve to try out because of another problem. A more important one. Your father. He would never allow you to be in a play. Never.

Well, she wouldn't have to bother him with it now. She might not make the cut. If she didn't, they'd have had an argument for nothing, and if she did, there would be plenty of time to discuss it with him then.

Chapter Six

It wasn't the female lead, but she had a few good speeches. She was going to play Carol, the part she had read for. Eve was thrilled. She felt as if everything were coming together in her life. She felt as if she were about to kick lose the restraints that had fastened themselves around her. In the past when she had ventured too far, she could always feel the bit tearing at her, but this time it was going to be different. She was different. Her father was different. At least she hoped he was. She would have to tell him about it now that her being in the play was a reality.

She looked up at the technical booth. Torbin was adjusting the lights. He smiled and waved at her. She waved back, then turned and walked away. He scared her a little, but she couldn't figure out exactly why. And she didn't have time to worry about it. At least that's what she told herself.

They were almost finished with a run-through of Act One. She looked at her watch and panicked. If she missed the five-thirty bus, she wouldn't make it home before her father, and he'd ask her where she had been.

She'd have to tell him. She wanted to tell him, of course. But not this way. When she was ready. Maybe tonight while they were cleaning up after dinner. That would be a good time. He'd be relaxed.

"Miss Raden," she said softly while the drama coach was going over her notes. "Do you mind if I run? I have to catch the five-thirty bus."

"No. No. Go on," Lisa Raden said absent-mindedly.

Eve grabbed her canvas bag and headed for the back of the auditorium. As she neared the exit, she jumped and caught her breath. Someone was sitting in the shadows.

Her eyes adjusted to the darkness, and she saw that it was Stephanie Brown.

"Stephanie," she said, surprised. "Are you working on the play?"

"Nah," Stephanie said, "just watching."

"You should have auditioned," Eve said. "I didn't think I'd get a part, but I did."

Stephanie laughed ironically. "I don't need to be in a play," she said. "My whole life's a drama."

"Yeah, I know what you mean," Eve said. But she didn't really know why she had said it. Because she knew what was going on in Stephanie's life, or because her life was sometimes a drama too?

"Well, I gotta run," Eve said, and she was almost relieved that she had an excuse to leave. "See you."

"Yeah," Stephanie said, bored.

Fine with me, Eve thought. I don't want to spend time with you either.

She ran to the bus stop and was glad to see two people still sitting there. She collapsed on the bench next to them.

"Hey, need a ride home?"

She looked up. Torbin was smiling at her. He was

always smiling at her. He was the happiest person she'd ever met. It made her a little nervous.

"Nope," she said. "Bus'll be here any minute."

"Come on," he said. "I'm going right past your house."

"You are?" she asked, surprised he knew where she lived.

"Sure."

"Okay," she agreed. "If it's not out of the way."

She followed him back to the parking lot and got into his VW Jetta, closing the door after herself.

"Okay, where to?" he asked.

"I thought you were going right past my house." She laughed.

"I am," he said, laughing with her. "Only you have to tell me where it is before I can go past it."

She liked him. She didn't want to like him. She looked for every excuse she could think of not to like the guy, but she liked him. She just didn't want to be disappointed. He was a freshman in college. She was only a junior in high school. He couldn't possibly be interested in her. He was just being nice to her. He was nice to everybody. Every time he looked at her, he probably remembered what idiots she and Binnie had been that night in Edy's restaurant. Talk about immaturity. She'd never done anything like that before, and she was sure she never would again.

Twenty minutes later they pulled up in front of her little two-bedroom house. She knew twenty minutes had passed because she checked her watch, but it had seemed like two. He was almost as easy to talk to as Tony, and Tony was the only guy she had ever felt comfortable with. Maybe because when she was with him Binnie was always there too.

"Listen," he said. "I know you'll probably think I'm just looking for an excuse to get inside your house, but

I really need to make a phone call. Could I possibly use your phone?''

"Sure,'' she said, laughing, "but we have to leave the front door open just in case you really are a wild man under that Mr. Nice Guy exterior.''

"Hey, you get what you see,'' he said as they walked to the house, "but your front door's already open.''

She looked in the driveway. Her father's truck wasn't there.

"This is weird,'' she said. "Something's wrong.''

"What do you mean?'' he asked.

They stopped walking.

"The door,'' she said. "It shouldn't be open.''

"Let's go next door and call the police.''

"No,'' she said. "If there's been a robbery, it's obvious they've already left.''

"I still think we should call the police,'' he said, concerned.

"Let's just walk up to the front door and look in first. Then we'll call the police if we have to.''

"Okay, but let me go. You stay here,'' he said, picking up a branch that had blown off the yucca tree.

Eve nearly laughed out loud. Because she was nervous and because he couldn't possibly defend himself from a kitten with a branch from a yucca tree.

Let it be a robbery, she said to herself as he moved up the walk. Just let it be that. But as Torbin walked to the front door, she knew that wasn't it.

"Eve,'' Torbin called out. "It looks okay to me. Maybe you just forgot to lock the door when you left this morning, and the wind blew it open.''

"Maybe,'' she said, joining him.

"We'll look around inside just in case,'' he said. "Just let me go first.''

She stood in the doorway as Torbin quickly walked through the house.

"All clear," he said, coming back to the front door. "I must have been right about the wind."

"Yeah, you must have been," she said, and she wanted to believe that, but as soon as she walked into the house, she could smell that strong, pungent, sickening odor of beer. It permeated the whole living room and burned her nostrils. She looked around. There were no beer cans in the living room. She was grateful for that, at least.

Torbin looked at her out of the corner of his eye. It seemed as if he wanted to say something, but he didn't. He just went into the kitchen and picked up the phone.

He must have smelled the beer too. That's why he had such a strange look on his face, she thought. She hoped he wouldn't ask her about it. She wished he'd just make his call and get the hell out of there so she could sort things out.

He came back into the living room, looking like his old self again. "Listen," he said. "Here's my phone number." He handed her a piece of paper with his number on it. "Just call me if you need—anything. I mean it. Anything," he said.

"Okay," she said, smiling weakly at him.

He started to leave. Then he turned back. "Maybe I'd better stay here until your mom or dad gets home," he said.

"No!" she said, almost shouting at him. "I mean, no, you don't have to do that. I'm fine."

"See you then," he said, putting his arm around her shoulders and giving her a hug.

Eve automatically stiffened when he touched her, and she immediately regretted it. But just like arm muscles, dormant feelings atrophy.

She went into her room and threw her things and herself down on the bed, preparing for her father to come home. She lay there for a long time, her eyes open but unfocused. She couldn't think. She recognized the old familiar feeling. The fog came down and folded itself around her like a protective blanket to prevent her from really seeing what was out there, when what was out there was too painful to see.

By seven-thirty, she had convinced herself that she had imagined the smell in the living room. Torbin hadn't mentioned it, after all, and he was not the type to keep quiet for propriety's sake. He would have made some joke about it, at least. She decided to walk back into the room and check it out.

The smell was gone. There was just a faint odor of something. It could have been anything, not necessarily beer. Her father would be home any minute, carrying a bag of groceries, singing "*La donna è mobile*" under his breath. He often stopped on the way home from work to pick something up at the store or to order food from a takeout restaurant.

She walked to the front door so she could open it and look down the street to see if his car was coming. But by the time she got to the door, she knew there was no reason to look out. His car probably wouldn't be coming down the street for a long time. She had taken off her shoes, and the bottoms of her feet were soaking wet. She took off her socks. They reeked of beer. That was why he had left the front door open. To eliminate the odor. He had obviously spilled beer on the floor, but he had been together enough to toss out the bottles and cans before he left. She didn't have to go out back and look in the garbage. She knew they'd be there.

Slowly, she made her way to the phone. Her arm ached as if it had just been broken again. Her head ached. A dull pain throbbed in her forehead between her eyes. She squinted and checked the list of numbers next to the phone. She coughed. This wasn't the first time she had had to call this number. She hoped no one was there so she wouldn't have to listen to stories she didn't want to hear.

"You have reached 118-2345. No one's in to take your message right now, but if you leave your name, number, and the time you called, we'll get back to you as soon as we get in, in the morning. If you have an emergency, you can reach us at this number—"

Eve hung up the phone. It wasn't an emergency—yet.

By nine-thirty she was hungry, so she made herself a salad and heated up some rolls, but when she sat down to eat, she felt sick to her stomach and threw the whole dinner in the garbage can.

By ten-thirty she began to pace the floor. Whatever he did, he was still her father, and he was still basically a good man. Even though she was mad as hell at him, she was worried about him too. She was more worried at this point than she was angry.

She fell asleep on the couch, and he woke her up when he came staggering in at midnight.

"Don't be mad" was the first thing he said before he collapsed on the wet floor. "Don't be mad at me."

She didn't say anything. She just tried to roll him away from the beer into a drier spot.

"They weren't doing as well as they expected," he said, slurring his words. "It's not that I did anything wrong. They liked my work. Said I was one of their best men. Reliable. Me. They said I was very reliable. And I was too. Never missed a day. Not a minute since I started there. But they had to lay off the last two people hired, and I was one of them."

He laughed. A horrible, self-pitying, self-denigrating laugh that sliced right through Eve's soul.

"You understand, don't you?" he asked. "You've got to understand."

She didn't want to make it any worse for him than it already was.

"Yeah. Sure," she said. "I understand." And on a certain level she did.

"I wouldn't have done it otherwise. You know that. I wouldn't have touched a drop. And this is it. I won't touch another one. Believe me," he said as he lay down on the floor.

"How can I?" she said under her breath.

"I'll make it up to you," he said as he passed out on the floor.

She brought a blanket from his bed and covered him, then she padded wearily into her room, turned off the lights, and covered herself, her body and her soul.

At two-thirty a strange noise startled her. She sat up, her ears alert. She heard it again. Burglars. She was sure it was burglars this time. Just as she had been sure it wasn't burglars before. Her heart started beating wildly, and her breath stuck in her throat. She had never been so scared in her whole life.

"Who is it?" she asked timidly, hoping her father would answer.

There was an eerie silence. She shivered and huddled down under the covers. If someone was there and she lay absolutely flat, smoothing the covers over her, they'd think her bed was empty. They'd search her room, maybe, but they wouldn't find much, unless they were interested in juggling. There was no jewelry, and she only had a few dollars in her wallet. But maybe they'd be mad if they couldn't find any money. Maybe they'd go on a rampage, ripping up everything, including the bed, and they'd find her, and then they'd really be mad. Or maybe they'd find her father passed out in the living room, and they'd— It was too horrible to think about. How many times had she used the expression "dead drunk"? Maybe he'd be a dead drunk. Maybe she wouldn't even care.

"Dad," she whispered.

No answer.

Boom, scrap, scrap, scrap. She heard the sounds again. She was sure this time. There was someone on the roof!

"Dad," she whispered again, her voice quavering. She had to get out of bed and wake him up. She didn't know what he could do to protect them, but that was his job, dammit—to protect her. She picked up Binnie's old baseball bat, which she had left at the house last week. Her legs felt like toothpicks, too weak to hold her up. She gripped the bat and moved as quickly as she could to her bedroom door. She stood in front of it for a moment, then opened it very, very quietly. She was shaking. She was hot and cold at the same time.

She looked into the living room. The light from the street lamp outside shone through the window. Her father still lay on the floor where she had left him. Nothing else had changed in the room.

Slowly she made her way over to her father. She shook him. "Wake up," she whispered.

He didn't move.

"Wake up," she said more urgently.

His snoring filled the room and sounded like trumpets in the quiet that surrounded them.

"Wake up," she said a third time. "Can't you see I need you?"

His snoring stopped for a moment as if he heard her in some distant fog. Then he continued snoring again.

Angry and frustrated, she kicked him, gently at first, then harder and harder. "I need you. I need you," she yelled, forgetting why she had tiptoed out there in the first place. "I can never count on you when I need you. Never. Never. Never," she cried, giving him one last kick.

This time he didn't even stop snoring.

Who cares what happens to me? she thought as she

walked back to her room. Who cares? I don't care. I hope some burglar does come in here. I hope he steals everything in the house. I hope he's a maniac, and he—

She wanted to cry. She wanted to cry so badly, but she couldn't. It would serve him right, she thought, slipping into bed. Then he'd be sorry. He'd really be sorry.

Boom, the sound again. This time right outside her window. They were coming in. She heard whoever it was land on the pavement. Then she heard a loud wail, like a baby crying, shrieking because its bottle had been taken away. It was the wail of a cat in heat.

She sank back against her pillow, relief flooding her body and flowing through her like a bolt of cleansing white energy. She felt alive again. But only for a moment. Following close on the heels of that relief was another emotion—resentment.

I'm not going to tell him about the play, she decided. Why should I? If he really cared about me, he wouldn't be lying out there now like some dumb dead animal. I'll tell him about it on opening night, she decided. Then it will be too late for him to do anything about it. And if he tries, she thought angrily, I'm out of here. I'm moving back to Delphi's.

Chapter Seven

"Don't be nervous," Torbin whispered.

"It's my big scene," Eve said.

"The play isn't opening for another two weeks. You still have time to work on it."

"But I'm not getting it. I'm just not getting it."

"You'll get it," he said reassuringly.

"I'm not sure I want to," she said finally.

"Yeah, I know what you mean," he agreed.

But she was sure he didn't know what she meant.

"Listen," he said, "I'm going to be in your neighborhood again after rehearsal, so why don't I drive you home?"

"Oh yeah, and what are you going to be doing in my neighborhood *this* time?" she asked, smiling at him, relieved to change the subject.

"Taking you home." He laughed. "Unless you'd let me take you out to dinner instead."

"Take me to dinner?"

"You do eat, don't you?"

"No, I mean, yes, of course."

"Of course you eat, or of course I can take you to dinner?"

"Of course I eat," she said. "I can't go to dinner."

"Okay. Some other time, then," he said, "but the ride's still on."

"I'll see you at the break," she said. "I'm going to go into the john and splash some water on my face, get ready for my big scene."

"Later," he said, climbing up to the lighting booth.

She walked to the john at the back of the auditorium. This time she wasn't surprised to see the shadowy figure sitting in the last row. She had gotten used to seeing Stephanie there. It was kind of weird, but for some reason she had never mentioned it to anyone. If Stephanie wanted to sit there during rehearsals, that was her business. Sometimes she remembered that Stephanie was out there, and she directed her speeches to her. It was kind of nice knowing she had an audience, even if it was an audience of one.

"How ya doing?" she asked as she passed by Stephanie quickly. She didn't really want an answer.

Stephanie raised her Coke bottle at Eve in response.

Eve went into the john. She looked at herself in the mirror. Boy, did she look tired. She was tired. On top of that she was totally stressed out. It was hard enough keeping up with schoolwork under ordinary circumstances. It was impossible with the play, and next week they would extend rehearsals until eleven or twelve o'clock. She'd have to arrange to stay at Delphi's on those nights.

God, look at those circles under your eyes, she thought. It looked at if someone had rubbed charcoal under her lashes. She looked like a gray-eyed owl. Even her blond hair hung limply to her shoulders, the body perm completely gone. "You are so ugly," she said out loud. She reached into her case, took out some cover-up, and smeared it over the pools of charcoal. She rubbed it in. That was a little better.

Of course, as if school and the play weren't enough to worry about, she had to worry about her father too. Though he'd kept his word, and he hadn't had anything to drink since the night he'd lost his job, she kept expecting him to slip. It broke her heart. Sometimes the aftermath was worse than the drinking itself. He'd be so pitiful the next day, trying to apologize without really saying he'd done anything wrong. They never really talked about it, just around it. Neither one of them said what they really meant. But they both knew there was something in the air between them, a tension that was like an old rope with each of them tied to the opposite end. The same rope that had kept them at a distance for the past few years. It was almost as if at the very minute there was a possibility for a relationship, one of them would do something so unforgivable they would each retreat into their separate corners, avoiding contact altogether.

He hadn't gotten another job yet, so she knew that any day—if not today, then tomorrow or the next day—it would be too much for him, and he'd go off on another bender. She swore that if he did, it would be the last one she would stay around to see. She couldn't take it anymore. She wanted her father back. She wanted him to be the gentle man he used to be—the daddy who made a crown of flowers for her hair and who sang her to sleep at night.

She walked out of the bathroom and back into the auditorium.

"You must really like this play," she said to Stephanie as she passed her.

"I'm waiting for your big scene," Stephanie whispered.

"What?" Eve asked, leaning toward her so she could hear better.

"Your big scene," Stephanie said, the unmistakable smell of cheap whiskey surrounding her mouth.

Eve stepped back so quickly she almost fell against the seat on the opposite aisle.

Stephanie just smiled at her and raised her Coke bottle again. "Cheers," she said. "I'll be watchin' you."

"Okay, gang," Lisa Raden said. "I think we should take a little break here before we get into Eve's big scene." She checked her watch. "Let's take fifteen."

Everybody started to get up and stretch. "Oh—one minute before you wander off," Lisa said. "I just wanted to let you know that permission slips went out yesterday, so they should have gotten to your houses today. Please, please have your parents sign them tonight and return them tomorrow. It's urgent. You can't stay for late-night rehearsals next week without written permission."

"Yeah, yeah," everybody said as they headed for the washrooms or for the soft-drink machines outside the theater. But Eve just stood there, staring at Lisa Raden.

"Permission slips," she said, "I didn't know anything about permission slips."

"I forgot you've never been in a play before," Miss Raden said. "School policy. No permission slips, no play. I usually get them out as soon as we begin rehearsals, but I sort of let it get past me this time."

"What if our parents won't sign them?" Eve asked.

"Sometimes parents get uptight about it," Miss Raden said.

Eve breathed a little more easily.

"But I just give them a call and explain why it's so important to rehearse right through the evening, and they always relent."

Eve stopped breathing altogether. Her arms and legs felt as if they had been planted in a cement block as she dragged herself slowly to the first row of seats and collapsed.

"Eve, come on up here," Torbin called from the control booth, but she kept her head down. She didn't want to look at him.

"Eve," he called more loudly. Then she heard him say, "Never mind. I'll come down."

By the time he climbed down from the lighting booth, it was almost all over. She sat there trembling, her whole body out of control. It had happened so fast, at first she thought she had dreamed it. But when she looked at Miss Raden's face, she knew she hadn't.

Out of the corner of her eye, she could see the rest of the cast and crew drawing back into the theater. She knew they all must have heard the explosion too.

Then a fog totally enveloped her, and she spaced out. She couldn't see or hear anyone. She just turned and walked out of the theater to the bus stop, without her coat, without her canvas bag, without a dime to take the bus.

The bench at the bus stop was empty, but it didn't matter. She'd wait there forever if she had to. She couldn't go back inside the theater. She sat down and automatically grabbed for her navy-blue canvas bag, but it wasn't there. She nearly choked with fear. She could face almost anything but the loss of that bag. Her whole identity was stuffed into it. She felt completely naked without it.

She was on the verge of tears when someone put a gentle hand on her shoulder. Her spine, which had been bent into a *C* as she slumped on the bus-stop bench, shot straight up like a steel post. She shrugged it off. It didn't matter whose hand it was. She didn't want anybody's pity.

"I brought your bag," Torbin said. "I thought you might need it."

She turned around to look at him.

"Thank you," she said softly.

"Come on," he urged. "I'll take you home. I told you I'd be in your neighborhood," he said, winking at her.

She wanted to be alone, but she found herself breathing more easily, for some reason. She could almost trust herself to speak. "But I won't be in my neighborhood," she said softly.

"Actually, I thought it might be a good time to drive over to UCLA and pick up some equipment we need to use for the play, but I can't carry it myself. How about coming with me?"

"Okay," she said reluctantly. After all, she didn't know where else to go at the moment, though she knew she'd eventually wind up at Delphi's house.

They drove in silence except for the radio, which Torbin kept low, as if he wanted to fill the space for her but didn't want to intrude on her private thoughts.

Forty-five minutes later, they pulled into the one empty metered parking space near the theater department building at UCLA. They got out of the car and walked through a path into the empty campus area. You could get lost here, she thought.

"I'm going to run in here," Torbin said, pointing to a nondescript-looking two-story building. "I have to talk to my tech professor for a minute. Why don't you walk over to the sculpture garden and look around? I'll meet you in front of the museum in fifteen minutes."

Her head was still swimming from what had happened at school. The fog prevented her from taking in exactly what Torbin was saying. She got the gist of it, but that was all. Something about a museum and a garden, but she wasn't sure what. He disappeared before she had a chance to ask him again. She sighed. It didn't matter. She walked along the path without noticing anything around her.

In a few minutes she found herself in a small plaza with a large building on one side and a smaller one in front of her. She walked to the smaller building. It was the museum. She decided she would stand and wait here for Torbin.

She leaned against the building and stared into space. Subliminally, she took in the trees and the flowers strategically placed around the area. Then her eye caught a huge sculpture almost directly in front of her. Even in her fog she could hardly miss it. She was drawn to it, though she had no idea what it was. She stared at it for a long time, and then as if it were magnetic, she found herself moving toward it against her will.

It dwarfed her, it was so large. It was a horizontal piece, abstract, yet representational enough for her to get a general idea of what it was. She walked around it, and it began to take shape for her. It really wasn't abstract at all. Not if you looked at it closely, as she was doing. It was two figures in flight. Soaring—or running away. She wasn't sure which. Running away, she decided. They were parallel to the ground, not pointed toward the sky. Yet there was some strange peaceful quality about the piece that calmed her down. Time had weathered the two figures to a rich, warm brown, and their connection seemed more than just physical. The smaller figure was on the back of the larger one, tightly clasping it. The two figures were so close together they were almost indistinguishable at first. It felt as if they shared some secret knowledge that was almost within Eve's grasp. The lines of the piece were so fluid and powerful that it made her feel almost powerful herself.

She walked around it again and again, taking in more details each time. The larger figure was a huge-breasted female. For some reason she longed to climb onto her back and replace the smaller one. She wanted to feel the smooth, hard metal against her body. She knew it would comfort her, guide her, maybe.

There was a plaque on the stone base of the sculpture. She bent over to look at it. "Mother and Child," it said.

She dropped back and froze.

Chapter Eight

She lay in the other twin bed in Delphi's room that night, listening to Delphi's breathing. The clock face stared her down hour after hour, and she knew there would be no sleep at all. She tried to blank out, to go peacefully into her private fog again, but this time she couldn't do it. The scene between her father and Miss Raden that had played itself out in the theater that afternoon continued to run itself through her mind over and over again. And it became clearer and clearer every time.

The pain that now stabbed her heart was far worse than the pain she had felt when she broke her arm. That time it had been an accident. He had chased her out of the house, but he hadn't planned to break her arm. She had fallen and broken it herself. This time he planned it. He had gotten into his truck and had driven to school, knowing all along exactly what he was going to say and do. Maybe it was partly her fault. Maybe she should have told him about the play, but he had never given her a chance to explain herself. He had made their private problems public, and she couldn't forgive him for that.

She knew he wouldn't be able to forgive himself either when he sobered up. If he remembered what he had done. If he allowed himself to remember. If he hadn't drunk himself into a total blackout before he got to school, so he'd be oblivious to everything, including the pain he had caused her and himself.

He was a private person too. He couldn't stand it when anyone suspected there was trouble at his house, or with him, or with his wife or daughter. That was one of the worst things for him when her mother left—that people knew.

No one at school knew he drank except her very closest friends, Binnie, Heather, and Delphi, and even they hadn't known for a long time. Or if they had, if they had suspected, they had never said a word, except among themselves.

Now everyone would know. There had been at least ten people in the theater besides Miss Raden, Torbin, and herself.

She tried to get the picture out of her head, but she kept seeing him standing there, the permission slip in his hand, shaking all over, the smell of booze so strong it seemed to fill the whole auditorium.

She had tried to say something to calm him down. She couldn't remember what. She had just wanted to get him out of there. But the words wouldn't come out of her mouth. They were stuck in her chest. They were still stuck there. She had sat planted in the first row while he ranted on and on. She had just sat there as if she were watching some bizarre play instead of witnessing her own destruction.

"I won't stand for this," he shouted, shaking the permission slip under Miss Raden's nose.

"What?" Miss Raden had said, confused.

"No daughter of mine is going to get up on a stage

and perform like a monkey so all the men in the audience can fantasize about her.''

"I'm sorry," Miss Raden had said calmly. "Do you mind telling me what you're talking about?"

Instead of pacifying him, Miss Raden's calmness made her father even more angry. He must have sensed that she was trying to take control of the situation, and he didn't want anyone else to be in control but him. This was his show. He would call the shots.

"Damn permission slip," he said. "I didn't even know she was in a play."

"Who?" Miss Raden asked. She had never met Eve's father.

"My daughter, that's who," he shouted at her. "Eve."

Miss Raden blanched.

"This is illegal. It's immoral," he yelled.

"Mr. Morrison," Miss Raden said softly. "I didn't know your family were fundamentalists. I didn't know it was against your religion for her to be in a school play."

"We're not any damn fundamentalists," he shouted. "This has nothing to do with religion. It has to do with morals."

"I don't understand," Miss Raden said. "I'm sorry."

"Of course, you don't understand," her father said, seething. "She's just like her mother. Wants to show off all the time. Have people look at her."

Eve slid further down into the seat. She had never wanted people to look at her. Even her juggling, she suddenly realized, was not a bid for attention, but a cover-up, a substitute for talking. If she juggled, she didn't have to talk. Juggling was communicating. If she juggled for someone, it meant she liked that person. She didn't have to say it.

Delphi had teased her once by saying that, for Eve,

juggling was foreplay. The rest of them flirted, teased, hung around with guys. Eve juggled.

"She's very talented, Mr. Morrison," Miss Raden said. "It's a talent that should be shared with other people."

"And don't I know what that means," her father said, laughing hysterically.

"What does it mean?" Miss Raden asked.

"It means you're a pimp," her father said, lashing out at Miss Raden. "It means you're putting her on display so some dirty old man can come along and offer her fame and fortune—a chance to *act*," he said sarcastically.

"Mr. Morrison, can we continue this discussion in my office?" Miss Raden asked, trying to take his arm and guide him out of the theater.

He pulled away from her. He wasn't finished yet. He didn't want to go into her office. He wanted to say what he had to say in front of Eve. Eve knew this instinctively. He was telling Miss Raden all the things he had kept inside himself all these years, things he had wanted to tell Eve but couldn't. Now he was telling her indirectly what he hadn't had the guts to say to her face.

"Act," he repeated. "Her mother did a real class job of acting. And isn't that what the so-called agent said to her—that she had a talent that should be shared with other people. She shared it all right. She really spread it around," he said, laughing with a laughter that hurt Eve so badly, she could feel it ripping through her.

"I'm sorry," Miss Raden said. "I don't understand."

"You don't understand much, do you?" her father asked.

"No, I guess I don't," Miss Raden said, "but I do understand that you're going to feel very bad tomorrow about what you're doing right now. And I'd like to stop you before you go any further.''

"I'll stop when I'm finished,'' her father said, swaying a little.

How much more could there be? Eve wondered. He had already destroyed her.

"A porno queen, that's where her mother's talent got her. She spread it around real good. Did you catch her Academy Award–winning performance in—"

"That's enough, Mr. Morrison,'' Miss Raden said, finally getting it together enough to stop him.

Eve didn't know what had happened next. It was at that point that the fog descended over her, and she ran out of the auditorium under its protective cover.

She turned away from the face of the clock and began to cry quietly. How could she go into the theater tomorrow after school and act as if nothing had happened? She couldn't face them—any of them. Especially Miss Raden. But she couldn't let them down either. The play was in two weeks. More important, she couldn't let herself down. Somehow she would go in there, and she would play her part so well everyone would forget she even had a father. Because that's exactly what she intended to do. Wipe him out of her mind and out of her life—forever.

I'm an orphan, she thought. I'm on my own.

Chapter Nine

The next day she drifted through school in a fog. She went to all her classes. She even answered a question in English, though she didn't know what she said. At lunch Delphi covered for her, sensing that she didn't want to explain anything to anybody. Delphi herself didn't know exactly what had happened in the theater the day before. Eve couldn't bear to tell her, and Heather, who was usually at the theater working on costumes, had been absent yesterday. The only thing she had said when she got to Delphi's house was that she needed a place to stay for awhile. Luckily Delphi's family was used to seeing her around, so they didn't ask questions either. And luckily she and Delphi were about the same size, so Eve could borrow her clothes. Of course she had her essentials with her in her trusty navy canvas bag. And she had her juggling balls, too, so there was no reason for her to go back home. None at all. Not even to look at the framed picture at the bottom of her drawer. She never wanted to see the face in that picture again. Not if what her father had said was true, and she knew it was. That's when he had the nerve to tell the truth. When he was drunk.

The hardest part was facing her now, though. She had to walk into the theater. She knew that just her presence would be enough to make everyone else totally uncomfortable. No one would know what to say to her. They'd probably be elaborately silent about what had happened yesterday, avoiding any reference to it at all, but that wouldn't make it any easier—she'd know what they were thinking.

She opened the door and stepped into the auditorium, giving herself a moment so that her eyes could adjust to the darkness. As usual, only the stage lights were up; the houselights were down. She looked around. Something was missing. At first she didn't know what it was. She just knew that something was different. Then she remembered. She looked along the seats in the back row, but they were all empty. It looked as if Stephanie had gotten tired of sitting through the rehearsals and had deserted them. For some strange reason, Eve was sorry she wasn't there.

The rest of the cast and crew were milling around the stage. A few of the actors were running through their lines together. Torbin was in the technical booth. Miss Raden was going over her notes from yesterday. Eve walked to the stage and jumped up. Suddenly everything got quiet. Miss Raden looked up from her notes.

"Listen, guys," she said. "I need to go over some stuff with Eve. Take fifteen."

She motioned for Eve to follow her to her office, which was in back of the stage area. Well, this wasn't going to be easy, Eve decided. She didn't know exactly what Miss Raden was going to say, but she knew it was going to be about her father. She'd probably try to get her to see the school psychologist or something. That's what teachers always did when they knew a kid was having a problem and they didn't know how to handle it themselves.

Whatever it was she was going to say, Eve hoped she'd just say it quickly and get it over with. If Eve didn't have to think about it, she'd be okay. At this point, she couldn't take back what had happened yesterday, but she could forget about it, if everyone else would.

"Want a cup of coffee?" Miss Raden asked when they got into her office.

"No, thanks," Eve said.

"Why don't you sit down, Eve," Miss Raden said, pouring herself a cup from a glass coffeepot sitting on an illegal hot plate on her desk.

"One of these days, Mrs. Lockshin is going to stop looking the other way when she comes in here," she said nervously, "and force me to get rid of my caffeine addiction."

Eve knew she wasn't nervous about the principal's taking away her illegal coffeepot. Miss Raden was nervous about the conversation they were about to have. Her nervousness put Eve more at ease. After all, what would she possibly hear that could be worse than what she had heard yesterday? And she had survived that, hadn't she?

"We have a problem, Eve," she said, without looking at her.

Eve didn't say anything. She didn't know what she was supposed to say. *We* have a problem? It seemed to her that *we* didn't have a problem. She did.

"I know how much this play means to you," she went on. "And it means a lot for us to have you in it. You're good. You're more than just good. You're very good. You've come a long way, and I think you'd go a lot further if you had the chance—"

"What do you mean, if I had the chance?" Eve asked, leaning forward.

"I just mean—"

"There's still two weeks until opening night," Eve said.

"Yes." Lisa Raden sighed. "Enough time for us to get your understudy in shape."

"But why?" Eve cried, getting up from her chair.

"No permission slip," Miss Raden said. "Without a permission slip, you can't stay to rehearse at night."

"No!" Eve cried. "Please!"

"I'm sorry," Miss Raden said. "I really am."

"Is that all you can say?" Eve asked. "Can't you do anything?"

"I tried calling your father this morning to see if he'd changed his mind—"

"Did you talk to him?"

"Yes."

There was a long silence.

"He was still drinking, wasn't he?" Eve asked.

"I'm sorry," Lisa Raden said again. "I seem to be saying that a lot lately, but I am sorry. I wish there was something I could do."

"Nobody'll know," Eve said. "Here—give me a slip, I'll sign his name to it. He'll never remember. If he throws a fit, I can just tell him he signed it during a blackout, and he forgot."

"I can't let you do that, Eve."

"Why not?"

"It's—it's just not right."

"Is it right to let him ruin my life like this?"

"No."

"Is that fair?" Eve whispered, her voice cracking.

"No, it's not fair," Miss Raden said. "Lots of things in life aren't right and aren't fair."

"Then let me sign it."

"Signing the permission slip isn't going to make it right." Lisa Raden sighed. "It'll be a Band-Aid for the moment, but that's all. It won't solve the bigger problem."

"I don't care about the bigger problem right now," Eve said. "I care about being in this play. It's the only thing I have to look forward to."

"Truth?" Miss Raden asked.

"Truth," Eve answered.

"I would have signed it myself." She sighed again. "But Mrs. Lockshin was in here first thing this morning. She didn't say anything directly. She just told me a story about a teacher who had forged a parent's signature once when her class was taking a bus trip to the museum and one of the students had forgotten his slip."

"It's not the same thing," Eve said.

"A drunk driver smashed into the bus, and five of the students were injured pretty badly," she went on. "One of the five was the student whose slip the teacher had signed. His parents sued the school district—and won. A lot of money."

"Thanks anyway," Eve said quietly as she got up and walked toward the door.

"Eve," Miss Raden called after her.

"Don't say you're sorry again," Eve said as she opened the door. "Just don't say you're sorry."

She left by the stage door so no one would see her walking out. She wandered over to the track. Delphi would probably be watching the meet. She might as well hitch a ride to her house with her. She was just too worn-out to take the bus, then hike the two miles from the bus stop to Delphi's.

She looked around. Delphi wasn't in her usual spot. She didn't see Binnie either, and she knew that Heather was in the theater working on costumes. She had caught a glimpse of her in the green room as she and Miss Raden had walked to Miss Raden's office.

"I won't say I know how you feel," Torbin said, walking up to her.

"Are you following me?" Eve asked.

"Yes," he answered simply.

"You don't know how I feel," she said. "No one does."

"You'd be surprised," he said.

"Nothing would surprise me anymore," she said.

"I don't believe that," he said, taking her hand.

She tried to pull away from him, but he held on to her with a firm grip.

"You have to work the lights."

"Sharon's working them for me," he said.

"Please let go of my hand."

"No," he said. 'Everybody needs a hand sometimes, and I'm going to give you one whether you want it or not."

"You're being presumptuous," she said.

"You're being stubborn," he said.

"If you don't like it, you can leave," she said, hoping he wouldn't, wishing she could really take his hand—take his heart too—but she was sure he wasn't offering her that.

"Okay, I will," he said.

Her heart sunk. Another loss.

But instead of walking away from her, he didn't let go of her hand. He pulled her along with him, and she let herself be pulled, pretending she didn't want to go, knowing that she needed to.

"I suppose you're going to be in Delphi's neighborhood again," she said, trying to be funny. But it had come out wistful instead.

"No," he answered. "I'm not going to be anywhere near Delphi's neighborhood. In fact, I live in the op-

posite direction. I was just going to drop you off at the
bus stop, and lend you a buck, maybe, if you needed
it for the bus.''

"Oh," she said, embarrassed.

"Disappointed?" he asked.

"No," she answered.

"Too bad," he said. "If you'd have been disappointed, I'd have had to cheer you up. I'd have taken
you to Haagen-Daz for ice cream. We could have sat
outside in the sun, eating our cones, soaking up the
rays—talking.''

"I was disappointed," she said slowly.

"Good," he said. "Let's go."

They sat in the sun, eating ice cream, just as he had
promised. The sun felt healing. Or maybe it was Torbin
who was the healer. He didn't ask her where it hurt, or
how it hurt, or how much it hurt; but he seemed to
know.

"Don't you ever go to classes?" she asked. She realized she didn't know very much about Torbin, except
that he was a freshman at UCLA, a theater major, that
he didn't live anywhere near Delphi, that he liked fifties
restaurants, and that he looked like Tom Cruise. She
also sensed a lot of other things about him, but she
didn't trust her senses yet. She didn't trust herself.

"My classes are over by two this quarter," he said.
"That's why I'm getting my tech credit out of the way
by volunteering at Belmont.''

"You're good," she said. "I heard Miss Raden say
you were a natural.''

"I am a natural," he said, laughing. "And it took a
hell of a lot of practice too.''

"Practice to be natural?" She laughed.

"Of course.''

"Natural means natural," she insisted, still laughing.
"It means that you don't have to work at it.''

"Really?" he asked, taking her hand again.

She wanted to pull away from him. She wasn't used to anyone touching her, and she didn't know how to respond. When he had dragged her along, holding her hand, that had been easy. She had pretended to resist. Now she didn't feel like resisting. She felt like holding his hand and not letting go. But she didn't want him to know that. She didn't want to give away anything else about herself. He already knew more about her than she cared to have anyone know. Especially somebody she lov— She gasped. The *L* word. She hadn't thought about it since her mother left.

"It's the most natural thing in the world for us to be sitting here talking," he said. "Agreed?"

"Agreed," she said.

"And eating ice cream?" he asked.

"Agreed," she said, smiling up at him.

"You're a great-looking girl, right?"

"I guess," she said, embarrassed.

"Right," he said emphatically. "In fact you're a knockout. That first time I saw you at Edy's, I'd have given anything to be Tom Cruise."

She blushed.

"And I'm a pretty good-looking guy, agreed?"

"Agreed." She laughed.

"Then why isn't it natural for us to be sitting here holding hands?" he asked, looking directly into her eyes.

"I don't know," she said, looking down.

"It isn't, though, is it?" he asked.

"No," she said, though she wished it could be.

"If we worked at it, it would be," he said.

She felt sad all of a sudden.

"I mean it. It might feel uncomfortable for a while, but if we practiced, it would be just as easy as—"

"Juggling," she said.

"Yeah, juggling," he agreed, without letting go of her hand. "Can you really juggle?"

"Want to see me?" she asked, getting ready to pull her hand away and get out her juggling balls.

"No," he said. "I believe you."

She was shocked. Everyone always wanted to see her juggle.

"Besides," he added, laughing, "I'd rather hold your hand."

The sun was long gone by the time they left the ice cream shop. He held her hand as they walked to the car. Maybe he was right, she thought. Maybe you did have to practice being natural. Holding his hand felt more comfortable already. He gave her hand a squeeze, and she squeezed his back. They must look like a real couple to people passing by. She wished her friends could see her now. She wished the whole world could see her.

"I'm not going to be able to see you for awhile," he said when they pulled up to Delphi's.

Her stomach sank.

"I can't come knocking on Delphi's door at midnight," he said, smiling at her. "Though I wish to hell I could."

She had forgotten about rehearsals. He'd have to be there from now till the end of the play.

"We're off on Sunday, though," he said. "Think you can get along without me till then?"

"No," she said, laughing, "but I'll try."

"I'm sorry about the play," he said finally.

It was the first time he had made any reference to what had happened to her today.

"Me, too." She sighed. "Me, too."

She was surprised at herself. Usually she wouldn't admit to anyone that something had disappointed her.

"And—about everything else too," he said.

"I know," she said, looking down.

He ran his finger along the side of her cheek, very, very softly, so that she wasn't sure he was really touching her at first. She leaned back against the seat and closed her eyes. Then she felt his lips on hers, very, very gently, like a spiderweb brushing against her.

Chapter Ten

"I'll call you tomorrow if I don't see you," he said as she opened the car door. She closed her eyes tightly for a moment after she got out of the VW.

"You don't have to make any promises," she said softly.

"What?"

"Nothing," she said. "See you around."

It was an old habit of hers, not wanting to hear any promises. Promises scared her. She used to count on promises. "We'll go to Disneyland on Saturday, I promise," her parents used to say. How many Saturdays had she sat home, all dressed and ready to go, anticipating every move she would make once she got to Disneyland? How many Saturdays had she sat in the living room in front of the TV, wishing time would speed up to double time so she could wake her parents and get them going? How many Saturdays had she put on the coffee, warmed up some rolls, if there were any in the house, and taken them breakfast in bed so they'd think she was a good kid and keep their promise? How many times had they looked at the breakfast and groaned,

"Get that out of here. Get that damn food away from me. I'm too sick to eat. Too sick to get out of bed today"? How many times had she walked out of their room, littered with wine bottles and beer cans, and into her own room, closing the door tightly behind her so she wouldn't hear them fighting when they finally did get out of bed?

And every time she blamed herself. Maybe she had made too much noise so they couldn't sleep. Maybe she shouldn't have brought them coffee. The smell made them sick. If she had just waited a little longer, they would have gotten up, and they would be on their way to Disneyland, but she had been too anxious. It was her fault. She had no patience. It was always her fault. They told her that, didn't they? Both of them. They said it more than once and in more than one way. And if they didn't say it, they thought it.

And if Torbin didn't call her again or see her again, that would be her fault too. It was her fault, after all, that she had gotten kicked out of the play, ruined it for everybody. Except maybe her understudy, Joy Ferguson, who would be more than happy to fill in for her.

If she had only told her father about it before he got the permission slip in the mail, it would have been all right. She had waited too long. No wonder he was in such a rage. She could understand it, in a way. He was her father. She made him look bad by not letting him know what she was doing.

No, she didn't really want to hear promises from anybody anymore. Promises put her on edge. It was hard, waiting for the minute they would be broken. The minute she knew the promise wouldn't be kept.

She was about to unlock the front door of Delphi's house when Delphi rushed out, almost knocking her over.

"What's going on?" Eve asked.

"What isn't going on?" Delphi shot back. "Mrs. Brown's having an hysterical fit in there."

"What else is new?" Eve asked. Mrs. Brown's hysterical fits were famous in the neighborhood.

"This one's worse than usual," Delphi said.

"What happened this time?"

"You see Stephanie at school, by any chance?"

"No," Eve said, remembering that she hadn't seen her sitting in the back row of the auditorium.

"Gone," Delphi said.

"Gone?"

"*Poof*—into thin air," Delphi said, raising her arms up.

"Kidnapped?" Eve asked. "Do they think she's been kidnapped?"

"No," Delphi said, wrinkling her forehead. "Nobody really thought of that, but I suppose it's a possibility."

"Well, she wouldn't have just vanished," Eve said.

"Yes, she would," Delphi said emphatically. "She's done it before, but just for overnight. This time she's been gone for four nights."

"Serious?"

"Damn serious," Delphi said.

"I saw her yesterday."

"Where?" Delphi asked, surprised.

"In the theater."

"That's really weird, 'cause she hasn't been to her classes for days, and she hasn't been home either."

"Where does she go?"

"Remember when we went to the Venice boardwalk on your birthday?"

"Yeah."

"Well—"

"Well, what?"

"Don't you remember seeing her there when we came

out of the shop where you got your Bruce Springsteen jacket?''

"Oh yeah," Eve said. "Yeah, I remember." Of course she remembered. She suddenly remembered more than she wanted to remember. She remembered seeing Stephanie, her eyes glazed, her hair matted, her clothes filthy, going up to a well-dressed young couple. She remembered seeing the woman open her purse, pull out some bills, and hand one to Stephanie. She remembered, all right. She remembered thinking for one terrible moment that maybe she'd have to live like that someday. From hand to mouth. Then she erased the thought from her mind. She'd never live that way. Never. Even if her father couldn't take care of her, she could take care of herself. She'd been doing it for years, hadn't she?

"I told her mother we saw her there," Delphi said.

"Did she call the police?"

"No."

"Why not?" Eve yelled.

"I don't know. I guess she doesn't want to admit that Stephanie has the same problems her brothers have," Delphi said.

"*Brothers?*" Eve asked. "She has more than one brother?"

"She has another older brother. Twenty-five."

"I didn't know that," Eve said.

"They're alcoholics," Delphi said.

"I'm sorry," Eve said softly.

"All of them."

"Maybe she just drinks," Eve said. "That doesn't mean she's an alcoholic, you know. If she just drinks sometimes."

"She doesn't drink just sometimes," Delphi said. "She drinks all the time. And she's been doing it for years."

"Come on," Eve said. "Years?"

"Years!"

"She's only sixteen," Eve said.

"Years," Delphi repeated.

"But you couldn't tell," Eve said, "till this year. She was always in the top classes and stuff."

"Kept it hidden from everybody until her brother got carted off," Delphi explained. "Then, I don't know, she just started drinking all the time. I don't know."

"So what's her mother doing?"

"Crying," Delphi said.

"And?"

"And nothing."

"Just crying?" Eve asked, bewildered. "Why doesn't she go look for her?"

"I don't know," Delphi said. "Maybe—maybe she doesn't want to find her."

"What!"

"I mean, maybe she thinks she wants to find her, but maybe she doesn't really want to find her."

"She's her kid," Eve said.

"Yeah," Delphi said.

"Of course she wants to find her," Eve insisted. "No mother in her right mind would just abandon her child like that."

"Maybe she's not in her right mind," Delphi said. "She thinks Stephanie's gone to find her older brother."

"Does she know where he is?"

"No, but she thinks Stephanie does."

"What a drag," Eve said, sinking down on the steps of the front porch.

"She won't admit Stephanie has a drinking problem," Delphi said. "She says her boys had problems, but not Stephanie. Stephanie was her only hope after her older brother disappeared and her other brother got locked up."

"So she's just going to ignore it?" Eve asked.

"I feel sorry for her," Delphi said. "And I feel sort of sorry for Stephanie too."

"I don't!" Eve said. "I don't feel sorry for either one of them."

"How can you say that?" Delphi said, looking down at her.

Eve knew what Delphi meant even though she didn't finish her thought. She meant that Eve, of all people, should be able to understand the problem since her own father was an—an—it was so hard for her to say the word, even to herself. Somehow it was easier for her to concede that he was a drunk than it was for her to admit that he was an alcoholic.

"Her mother said Stephanie doesn't have a real problem. She just drinks wine," Delphi said, almost with a laugh, as if it was the stupidest thing she'd ever heard.

"Wine?" Eve repeated.

"As if wine couldn't get you just as drunk as anything else," Delphi said.

"She drank wine," Eve said almost to herself.

"Kept a bottle in her locker at school," Delphi said. "I saw it when it fell out once and smashed all over the floor."

Eve got up from the steps and started walking down the driveway.

"Where are you going?" Delphi called after her.

Eve didn't answer. Delphi's voice was curling around her head, but it seemed to be coming from somewhere in the distance.

"She drank wine," Eve said. She'd walk into her parents' bedroom after school, throw down her books, and lie across the unmade bed, looking up at her mother.

"Have a good day?" her mother would ask, absentmindedly.

Sometimes Eve would talk on and on, telling her mother about what had happened in school, but often she'd stop in the middle of a sentence, embarrassed, knowing that her mother hadn't heard a word she had said.

After a short silence, her mother would turn around to look at her and say, "That's nice." Then she'd turn back to her mirror. She liked to fix herself up in the afternoon. Eve thought it was wonderful that her mother wanted to look nice for her father when he came home from work.

Eve liked to watch her mother at her dressing table. Her mother would pick up the bottle of dark red wine and pour it into a glass with a long, long stem. A goblet, her mother called it.

"When I'm rich and famous," she used to say, "I'll drink champagne every day, from fluted goblets that cost fifty dollars apiece. And when I finish the bottle, I'll toss it away and then I'll break the glass against the wall for good luck," she'd say, laughing, and Eve would laugh with her, though she couldn't imagine why anyone would get pleasure out of throwing an expensive wineglass against the wall and breaking it.

Sometimes her mother would drink a whole bottle of wine while she sat in front of her table, and her face would flush with excitement, and she'd get up and dance around the room, picking Eve up from the bed and making her dance around the room with her.

Eve would protest, of course, but she loved it. She loved dancing around the room with her beautiful mother. It didn't matter that she slurred her words or that she didn't pay any attention to Eve. The only thing that mattered was that her mother was happy and that she was dancing around the room holding her. It almost didn't matter that the dancing would sometimes make her mother too dizzy to make dinner, and Eve would have to go to the store, buy some ground beef and potatoes, and get dinner on the table herself. It didn't matter that she was only eight or nine years old.

And it didn't matter if her mother sometimes got too sick from all the dancing around to come to the table after Eve had made the dinner. It really didn't matter that often she'd have to eat it by herself.

What mattered was the way her mother would smile at her and pat her on the head the next day and tell her what a great kid she was for taking care of everything.

Sometimes she wished her mother wouldn't pour so much wine into her glass. Sometimes she watched it flowing out of the bottle, all over the dressing table, and she thought it was blood, her blood, that her mother had drained out of her body and was drinking as she put on her makeup and became an entirely different person.

"Eve," Delphi said, running up behind her. "What's wrong?"

"She drank wine," Eve said, staring straight ahead. "She only drank wine."

"It's a disease," Delphi said.

"A disease?" Eve said, laughing, though the laughter was the kind that hurt, not the kind that liberated.

"Yeah. That's what my mom told Mrs. Brown. That alcoholism is a disease."

"Then why do people infect themselves over and over again, if it's a disease?" Eve shouted. "Nobody deliberately goes out and gets cancer, or has a heart attack, or gets AIDS," she yelled. "Those are diseases. Drinking is—" She was so angry, she could barely control herself.

"God, don't take it so personally," Delphi said. "You don't even know her that well."

"I thought I knew her," Eve said softly. "I thought I knew her, but I didn't really know her at all."

Chapter Eleven

She wasn't going to go. She told Torbin that she just couldn't, and he understood. Up until the last minute, she thought she'd stay at Delphi's and watch TV with Delphi's little brother. But Heather had called and asked if she needed a ride. Heather just assumed she'd want to go, and to her surprise, Eve found herself saying yes, she did need a ride.

But Heather had run off as soon as they got to the theater. She had to check the costumes, make sure that everyone was dressed and ready to go, that there were no last-minute seams to adjust or hems to straighten.

She wandered around in the empty auditorium feeling very much alone, and very sorry she had come. She looked up to the lighting booth, hoping to catch Torbin's eye, but he was checking everything out and giving Sharon last-minute instructions. She didn't want to get in the way. She'd see him at intermission.

What am I doing here? she asked herself. Am I some kind of masochist or something? I'm not that good a sport. I can't pretend it doesn't matter to me that someone else is going to be up there tonight saying my lines.

I should go into the dressing room and see if they need help with makeup or costumes, but it's too hard being backstage if your heart is in the part you *want* to play and not in the one you're *forced* to play.

Something had happened to her in the past few weeks. She didn't know what exactly. But she knew she didn't want to smile and pretend everything was all right when it wasn't. She didn't want to juggle, to keep herself from facing feelings. She wanted to break through the fog and find out who she really was. She knew she had to do that if she and Torbin were going to have any kind of relationship. He simply was not the kind of person to let her get away with pretense of any kind.

It was painful looking at herself. She didn't like everything she saw, but she was trying to be as honest with herself as she could be, taking one step at a time. There were still some things she couldn't deal with, couldn't think about, or confront in any way. But she was making a start.

She sat down in the back of the auditorium trying to examine why she had come, and she decided that, in fact, there were lots of reasons. She had come because she was hoping for a miracle, even though she didn't really believe in miracles. She was dreaming, wishing, hoping, praying—that Joy Ferguson would fall into a faint before the play began, right before it began, and that Heather would run up to Miss Raden and tell her that Eve was in the theater, and she could take over for Joy.

She would, of course, do a fabulous job, and everyone would want her to continue in the role every night, but she would be magnanimous. Opening night would be enough for her. She would turn the part back over to Joy, who would have recovered from whatever it was that had affected her almost immediately. Joy, thrilled with Eve's graciousness, would insist that they share the role. She would do it one weekend, and Eve the next.

Eve sighed. So much for miracles. The lights were up in the theater and it was filled with faculty, parents, and other students. She checked her watch. If Joy was going to faint, she'd better do it quickly, or Eve wouldn't have enough time to get into her costume before the curtain went up.

She looked up at the lighting booth again and caught Torbin's eye. He raised his fist in a salute to her. That was another reason why she had come. Because of Torbin. Because she wanted to show him she was tough. No, she corrected herself. That wasn't it. He knew she was tough. What he didn't know was that she was only tough on the outside. Even if she couldn't cry, she could feel. She could feel pain just as strongly as anybody else, stronger maybe. Which was why she always let the fog wrap itself around her, to stop the pain when it became too much for even her to bear.

Maybe she'd tell him about it someday. Somehow she knew if anyone could understand her, it was Torbin. And lately she felt as if she really needed to be understood. Even though Delphi, Binnie, and Heather knew her, had known her for so many years, they didn't really *know* her. They couldn't. Their lives were so different from hers. They were so free. Having someone to depend on makes you free, Eve thought, sitting there. She had never had anyone to depend on except herself. Sometimes when they were all at Binnie and Heather's or at Delphi's, laughing and talking, listening to music, doing crazy things, she'd feel like bursting into tears. For no reason, really, except that she'd think that this was her family. Except they weren't really her family, and if they all got mad at her for some reason or moved away, she'd be out there by herself, alone.

She didn't want to be alone. Alone was suddenly too

lonely. It hadn't always been lonely. She used to have so many things to fill her time. But when she stood facing herself now, she had to admit that she was alone and lonely. Maybe she was lying to herself. Maybe she always had been. She had not spoken to her father for two weeks, though he had called Delphi's every day. She had cut him out of her life, knowing how much it would hurt him, but what she hadn't counted on was how painful it was for her. After her anger had subsided, there was the terrible emptiness that yawned inside of her like a chasm too big to ever be filled by anyone or anything.

She was glad when the houselights went down. She didn't want to smile at anyone. She held on to her program with her name scratched out and Joy's written in. She squirmed in her seat, waiting for Joy to appear on stage, waiting for her big scene.

Before the final speech, Eve leaned forward in her seat, straining so she wouldn't miss a word. She mouthed each syllable with Joy, her whole heart and soul in the part. She didn't know if Joy felt it as she did or not. It didn't matter. She only knew that when *her* character, Carol, talked about going off the cliff in the car, when *her* character talked about her own death, Eve understood exactly what she was saying. She was saying that dying was more than breathing your last breath. You could live your life as a somnambulist, a zombie, walking around as if you were alive—walking around in a fog. And maybe that was a more horrible kind of death.

When the curtain came down, and the cast took their curtain calls, and signaled for Miss Raden to join them so they could give her flowers and hugs and kisses, Eve felt drained. She felt as if she had been on stage every minute of that play even though she had never left her seat.

Eve didn't know if Joy was good or not. She wasn't listening to her. She was silently speaking every one of Carol's lines and giving the role everything she had. She had put herself in Joy's place.

Torbin pulled her up from her seat.

"I'm so glad you came," he said, giving her a hug.

Everyone in the theater hugged all the time. It was something she just couldn't get used to. When they tried to hug her, she'd back away, juggling whatever she could get her hands on, or she'd pretend she didn't know what they were going to do, and she'd move to the side or turn around, just in time to avoid their touch.

But she didn't back away from Torbin. She had gotten used to holding his hand. She dreamed about the night he took her home and kissed her so lightly she thought she might have dreamed that too. Maybe she'd get used to his hugging her. It didn't mean anything to theater people, she kept telling herself. It didn't mean anything to Torbin. He was hugging her just as he had hugged Joy and Heather and Miss Raden, and the rest of the cast and crew.

"You're coming to the cast party with me," he said. "I was going to drive over to Delphi's to pick you up, but this is much better." He laughed, pulling her back-stage with him.

"No!" she protested. This was testing her strength to the limit.

"No is not in my vocabulary tonight," Torbin said. "Come on backstage. There's a surprise party. Sort of a preparty party."

"For who?" Eve asked.

"Me."

"Then how can it be a surprise?" Eve laughed.

"How can anything be a surprise around the theater?'' he said, shaking his head. ''Everybody knows everybody else's business.''

''Yeah,'' Eve said. ''That's exactly what I was thinking. I can't go back there.''

''Then I can't either,'' he said.

She turned her head and rolled her eyes. The last of the audience was drifting out to the lobby.

''Stephanie!'' she cried.

''Come on,'' he said. ''I know there are some weird people in the theater department, but I have no intention of undergoing a sex change for you, or anybody else. Even though I'd walk on water if you asked me to,'' he said, chucking her under the chin. ''At least I'd try.''

''Stephanie Brown,'' she said, wrinkling her forehead. ''She's been missing for two weeks. I saw her. She just walked out of the theater.''

''Then she isn't missing anymore,'' Torbin said flippantly.

''No,'' Eve said. ''I mean it. She has been missing.''

''Maybe she was sick,'' Torbin said.

''She was sick all right,'' Eve said. ''I think I ought to call her mother.''

''Come on, there's a phone in Lisa Raden's office.''

''There's one outside the theater too,'' Eve said.

''Okay.'' He sighed. ''If you won't come to my surprise party, then I won't go either, and that'll be one hell of a surprise.''

''You have to go,'' Eve said. ''Go on. I'll wait for you in your car, if you want me to.''

''Nope,'' he said. ''I refuse to go without you.''

''Torbin,'' she wailed ''You have to go. It's for you.''

''But I'll be worrying about you,'' he said. ''Is she really waiting for me in my car, or did she take off with some surfer?''

''You're crazy,'' Eve said, laughing.

"So what else is new?"

"All right," she said. "Let's go make the call first, then I'll go to your unsurprise party with you, but I want you to know that I don't really want to go, and I'll feel like a total jerk."

"Good," he said. "Then we'll feel exactly the same way. Do you have any idea how stupid I think surprise parties are? Especially when they're for me."

Miss Raden unlocked her office door for them, and they both went in. Eve was so preoccupied thinking about Stephanie, she didn't even realize that this was the first time she had seen Miss Raden since the last time she was in this office, the day she had been replaced by Joy Ferguson.

She called information for Stephanie's number and quickly wrote it down. Then she dialed, hoping Mrs. Brown was home so she could get rid of the responsibility of knowing Stephanie was out there. She wanted to share that with somebody else. Somebody more responsible than she wanted to be.

There was no answer. No answering machine, either. "Damn," Eve said. "Now what do I do?"

"You did what you could," Torbin said.

"But—"

"Eve," he said, taking her hand. "You did what you could. You don't have to save the world. You don't have to make it right for everybody."

"Me?" she asked, surprised. "I'm not like that."

"Of course not," he said. "Now just come into the green room with me and prove it."

"What a guy," she said, letting him pull her along.

"Surprise," everybody yelled when they walked into the green room.

She hoped Torbin would act surprised even though she knew he hated being a phony. Everyone would be disappointed if he didn't.

"Surprise," Torbin said.

What a strange reaction, she thought. Oh no—he means surprise that he brought her to the party. Everyone was staring at her, wondering why she was there. God, why had she let him talk her into this? Why couldn't the floor just open up and let her drop through it? This was so embarrassing. It wasn't enough that they had all seen her father's class act. Now she had to stand there like an idiot while they saw hers too.

"We weren't sure you'd come," she heard Miss Raden say somewhere in the fog. "But we appointed Heather to get you here any way she could."

Eve heard Heather's giggle coming from somewhere to her left. How could one of her best friends betray her like this?

"Anyway," Miss Raden went on, "we just wanted you to be a part of this opening night too, Eve, because we really couldn't have done this play without you."

"But I wasn't even in it," Eve heard herself say.

"You understood your character in a way that even I didn't understand her," Lisa Raden said. "You brought a whole new dimension to the part, and we all understood her so much better because of you."

"It was Joy's idea to thank you," Torbin said, pointing to the cake.

"What?" Eve said, very confused by the commotion going on around her. Why were they talking about her at Torbin's surprise party?

"So," Miss Raden said, "thanks from all of us."

Everyone was clapping and trying to hug her. Had they all gone out of their minds? She turned to look at Torbin, who was laughing his head off. "Surprise," he said for the second time.

"Torbin, I don't understand," she said.

"Just cut the cake," he said, walking her over to the makeup table, which held an enormous cake with theater masks on it and strawberries spelling out, "Thanks Eve."

Torbin put the knife in her hand. She looked at him and shook her head. "I can't believe this," she said. "You hate surprise parties. Especially if they're for you."

"Well"—he laughed—"I had to say something, didn't I?"

"I am never going to believe anything you say again," she said, cutting the first piece of cake.

"I hope not," he said. "I'm a notorious liar. I'd hate to spoil my reputation."

Chapter Twelve

"It was a surprise, right?" he asked as they walked out of the theater to the parking lot.

"It was a real surprise," she said softly. She was unexpectedly choked up.

"So—glad I talked you into coming?"

"Yeah, I'm glad," she said. Everyone had been so nice to her. She had been the center of attention for a-while, and she hadn't even been juggling. Everyone just wanted to say hello and tell her they were glad she had been a part of the play even if she hadn't been able to show an audience what they had seen during rehearsals.

"I can't believe you guys did that for me," she said as Torbin unlocked the car door.

"Wait a minute. I'll unlock your side," he said, leaning over.

"It's open," she said, noticing the button was up.

They got into the car and looked at each other. It was the first time they had been alone in two weeks. They had caught glimpses of each other after school when Torbin came for rehearsals, and they had talked on the phone, but aside from one Sunday when they had gone to the Museum of Contemporary Art and had been alone in the car coming and going, this was the first time they weren't surrounded by other people.

"It's going to be strange not being here every afternoon," he said, taking her hand.

She had forgotten Torbin would be gone after the play closed. She wondered if she would be forgotten too. He'd be back on campus. He wouldn't want to spend time with a high school student.

"I'll still have my afternoons free, though, so I can come by and pick you up sometimes—after I get caught up on all the work I've let slide this quarter."

Yeah, sure, she thought. He'll be gone from here, and that will be that.

"You're so beautiful," he said, as if he were looking at her for the first time.

She blushed. "I told you before I'd never believe anything you said again," she said, but she wanted him to think she was beautiful, even though she knew she wasn't. Maybe then he would want to see her again.

He touched her face very gently, as if he knew she would back away if he moved in on her too quickly. "Your skin is so soft," he said, moving closer to her.

Her breath was caught in a ball of gauze and bounced against her chest, then it jumped back and forth from her throat to her stomach in tiny leaps. He touched her face with both his hands and the ball became harder. It pounded faster and faster. She wanted to match him point for point. She wanted to put her hands on his face. She wanted to feel his lips on hers again. She wanted him to take her in his arms.

But she was afraid.

If she let go—if she turned off the committee in her head, which continually told her what to do—she might go too far. After all, he was a college student. Only she wished this one time the committee would just shut up and let her do what she wanted to do. She wanted to touch him. She wanted him to touch her, not just on her face.

He leaned over to her and began to stroke her hair, his face close to hers. Almost involuntarily she put her arms around his body and let her head drop to his shoulder. They were so close.

She heard a strange moan. She held her breath and stiffened.

"What's the matter?" he whispered.

"Nothing," she whispered back, confused.

Then she heard it again.

"Are you okay?" he asked, sitting up.

Suddenly she realized the sound wasn't coming from Torbin. "That wasn't me," she said.

At the same time they looked in the backseat. Stephanie Brown was on the floor, wedged between the front seat and the backseat.

"Oh my God," Eve cried, leaping out of the car, throwing back the front seat so she could get to Stephanie. Torbin lifted her gently onto the backseat.

"Stephanie," Eve cried. But Stephanie lay limp, saliva drooling from the side of her mouth.

"Is she breathing?" Eve whispered, holding her own breath.

"She's breathing," Torbin said, picking up an empty plastic bottle. "Valium," he said, reading the label in the light from the street lamp. "A prescription made out to Janet Brown."

"Her mother," Eve said.

"And here's an empty bottle of wine," Torbin said, reaching down to the floor of the backseat.

He handed both the prescription bottle and the empty wine bottle to Eve. "Here, we'll take these in with us so they'll know what she's swallowed," he said, getting into the car.

* * *

They pulled up to the emergency unit of Central Hospital and told a guard what had happened. An orderly was out in no time with a gurney. He lifted Stephanie onto it and wheeled her in. "Follow me," he said to them curtly.

They gave the receptionist all the information they could and handed her the two bottles, which she immediately passed on to the resident who was on his way into the cubicle where they had taken Stephanie.

"I don't know her phone number," Eve said. "But it's listed in information. I called her house earlier."

The receptionist got in touch with Stephanie's mother, and Eve and Torbin sat down in the waiting room to wait for her.

Mrs. Brown hadn't arrived yet when the resident came over to them.

"I'm Dr. Miller," he said quietly.

Torbin and Eve introduced themselves.

"Do you know what happened?"

"Not exactly," Torbin said, "but we can put two and two together. Is she going to be all right?"

"Luckily, you got her here in time," Dr. Miller said.

"What did you do?" Eve asked.

"We pumped her stomach," Dr. Miller said. "Not a pretty sight, but then a suicide attempt is never very pretty."

Eve shivered. He said the word—just like that. The word she and Torbin had kept themselves from saying all the way to the hospital.

"You can see her if you want to," Dr. Miller said. "I think it would be good for her if you went in—so she'd know someone cares about her. That's important right now."

Neither Eve nor Torbin moved.

"You don't have to stay long. Just let her know you're there," Dr. Miller said.

"I'll go," Eve said, walking toward the cubicle.

Stephanie was very pale, and a charcoal liquid was oozing out of her mouth.

Dr. Miller wiped it away. "We administered a chemical compound to her stomach after we pumped it," he explained. "To flush out anything that might be left in her system."

Stephanie tried to smile at Eve, but she couldn't quite make it.

Eve was too nervous and scared to speak. She just stared at Stephanie. Stephanie tried to lift her hand toward Eve. Eve walked over to the bed and took it in hers.

"I don't understand," Eve whispered.

"I didn't think I would die," Stephanie said so softly Eve could barely hear her. "I wanted to die, but I was afraid," she said. "I didn't want to live anymore, but I was too scared to die."

Eve bit her bottom lip. She knew exactly what Stephanie meant.

"The committee in my head told me to do it," Stephanie whispered. She was hoarse from the tube that had been injected into her throat.

"Don't talk," Eve said, holding her hand tightly.

"I want to talk," Stephanie said. "Or I'll die." She started to cry. "I don't want to die. I just wanted her to look at me."

"Who?" Dr. Miller asked. Eve knew the answer before Stephanie said another word.

"My mother," Stephanie said.

"Get some rest now, Stephanie," Dr. Miller said, putting his hand on her forehead. "Your mother will be here pretty soon, then we can decide whether to send you home or to admit you."

Eve walked out of the room with Dr. Miller. "I may need your help," he said. "Do you know the mother?"

"A little," Eve said.

"Stephanie is going to wind up in here again unless she gets some help," Dr. Miller said. "I've seen it a million times."

"What do you mean?" Eve asked.

"I want to admit her to the CCD program at the hospital."

"Won't she go?"

"I think she will, but I'm not sure her mother will let her."

"A chemical dependency program?" Eve asked.

"Yes."

"Why wouldn't her mother let her?"

"A hunch. We'll see. Will you stick around and help me convince her?"

"I'll stick around," Eve said, "but I don't know if it'll do any good."

As they walked into the waiting room, Mrs. Brown came bursting in, her suede coat flying in the wind she created as she swung through the revolving door.

"I'm Janet Brown," she announced, looking around for someone in charge.

Dr. Miller introduced himself and told Mrs. Brown what had happened.

"We'll have our family doctor look at her immediately," Mrs. Brown said, almost defensively.

"That's a good idea," Dr. Miller said.

"I have the car out front. I've already called him. He's going to meet us at St. Luke's. He's on staff there."

"Mrs. Brown," Dr. Miller said gently. "I think Stephanie should stay here."

"I told you our doctor is at another hospital."

"I think she needs more help than your doctor can

give her. She needs to go into a program. We have one of the best ones in the country here.''

"What kind of program?'' Mrs. Brown asked hostilely.

"For chemical dependency.''

"For alcoholics,'' Mrs. Brown said. "Forget it. She's not an alcoholic. I should know. I have two sons and an ex-husband who are. She just wanted attention,'' Mrs. Brown said bitterly. "Well, she'll get her attention, but it won't be in any detox program for eight or ten thousand dollars.''

"Your insurance might cover some of the cost,'' Dr. Miller said.

"They're not locking her up in here,'' Mrs. Brown said. "So they can get her to tell them what a lousy parent I am, what a terrible family life she's had. I've had enough of that to last me a lifetime. I'm just not going to go through that again.''

"Mrs. Brown,'' Eve said quietly, "Stephanie tried to kill herself. She didn't want to live anymore. This time she said she was afraid to die, but if she ever gets too drunk to be afraid, maybe next time she'll finish the job.''

Mrs. Brown looked at Eve for a long moment. Eve thought she was going to slap her across the face for being so outspoken.

"Who are you?'' Mrs. Brown asked finally.

"Eve Morrison. I'm staying with Delphi's family.''

"Oh yes,'' Mrs. Brown said. "You're the girl whose father is an alcoholic.''

The words stunned Eve. She choked and looked away from Mrs. Brown and Dr. Miller.

"Talk to her,'' Torbin said, joining the group. "Just talk to her. Ask her what she wants to do.''

"I don't care what *she* wants to do,'' Mrs. Brown said. "She's given me nothing but trouble since her brother left. I've got enough on my mind worrying about him. If she needs to see somebody, I'll take her to see somebody, but a program is out of the question.''

"Because they'll want to see you too?'' Torbin asked.

"No,'' Mrs. Brown hissed. "Yes,'' she stammered.

"Talk to her,'' Dr. Miller said, leading Mrs. Brown to Stephanie's cubicle.

"I tried to be a good mother,'' Mrs. Brown said as she walked away, tears rolling down her face.

Chapter Thirteen

Eve was pretty shaken up by the time she got back to Delphi's. There were more issues involved in Stephanie's suicide attempt than she wanted to deal with at the moment, but after she told Delphi and her family what had happened, she was forced to confront the issue she had been trying so desperately to avoid.

"Look, honey," Delphi's mother, Mrs. Decopolis, said after Delphi, her brother and father had gone up to bed. "I know this has been very hard for you."

"I can handle it," Eve said as she began walking out of the room.

"I know that," Mrs. Decopolis said, "but sometimes it's good to talk to someone, not keep it all bottled up inside of you. That's what Stephanie tried to do, I think."

"I'm not an alcoholic, Mrs. Decopolis," Eve said defensively. "I'm not going to drink myself into oblivion. I won't try to commit suicide," she added. "Don't worry."

Eve was afraid that Delphi's mother would change her mind about her staying with them. Maybe Stephanie's suicide attempt would force her to face the fact that she had taken in some stray who might cause her the same kinds of problems Stephanie was causing her mother, problems nobody needed, especially when it wasn't even your own kid. Eve had to convince Mrs. Decopolis that she was strong enough to stand on her own two feet, no matter what.

"I'm not worried about that," Mrs. Decopolis said. "I've known you for a long time, Eve. I know that you're one hell of a strong kid. But I also know that you haven't said one word about your father since you walked through that door weeks ago. When I tell you he called, you just stare at me blankly. I'm not even sure whether you hear me or not."

"I hear you," Eve said.

"You look as if you're in another world sometimes," Mrs. Decopolis said gently.

"I hear you," Eve said more insistently. She didn't want to put up with Mrs. Decopolis's third degree right now. All her life she had put herself on trial, and she always found herself guilty—of everything. She didn't need the same verdict from the judge and jury.

"I don't think you can avoid thinking about your father, Eve," Mrs. Decopolis said quietly. "I know you want to—"

"I think about him," Eve said, interrupting her.

"I mean, you have to think about how you're going to handle this," Mrs. Decopolis said, clarifying herself.

"I'm not going to," Eve said, as if that were a decision Mrs. Decopolis could live with.

"He's willing to do whatever you want him to," Mrs. Decopolis said, "but he wants to talk to you."

"No!" Eve said. "I'm not going to talk to him."

"He's your father, Eve."

"Then why doesn't he act like a father?" Eve said.

"He told me what happened," Mrs. Decopolis said. "I'm sorry."

"I know you're sorry. He's sorry. Miss Raden's sorry. Everybody's sorry. But that doesn't change what happened. Okay? That doesn't cut it."

"I understand," Mrs. Decopolis said.

"No, you don't," Eve said. "You do not understand. Everybody and his brother thinks they understand. They're sorry and they understand. Look, I appreciate your letting me stay here—"

"You're like part of our family, Eve—"

"Yeah—I'm *like* part of your family, only I'm not your family," Eve said, "so I appreciate your letting me stay here."

"It's okay," Mrs. Decopolis said.

"Only, I won't talk to him. Nobody can make me."

"Then just talk to me about it."

"No. I don't mean to offend you, but no. I just want to forget about him, pretend he doesn't even exist. He doesn't exist for me anymore. Maybe it's my fault. Okay, I admit it. It is my fault. A lot of it. But I can't change, and he won't change, so we're just going to keep hurting each other for the rest of our lives. There's nothing to talk about. See?"

"Maybe if you talked to him with somebody else—"

"Look, I know what he'll say, and I'll wind up feeling guilty and terrible for hurting him. And I'll move back to my house, and it'll just start all over again."

"Maybe it would be different this time."

"Maybe and maybe not," Eve said wearily.

"I'm not going to push you," Mrs. Decopolis said.

"Thank you," Eve said, walking to the door.

"I'm here for you, Eve," Mrs. Decopolis said.

"If you're really here for me," Eve said, "tell me how I can just get him out of my life for good." In her own mind she finished the thought. Get him out of my life for good so I won't have to wind up in the hospital with him like I did with Stephanie. I just can't go through that. No matter how strong I am, that would kill me too.

"There is a way," Mrs. Decopolis said slowly.

Eve turned around to look at her.

"What way? Have you adopt me?" she asked, half joking.

"Not exactly," Mrs. Decopolis said. "I'm sure your father wouldn't permit that. It would be too threatening, too painful for him. But he did say he'd do whatever was best for you. Maybe it would be best for you to declare yourself an emancipated minor."

"I am an emancipated minor," Eve said. "I don't have to declare it."

"I mean legally," Mrs. Decopolis said.

"Legally?"

"Your father would have to agree. He'd have to sign the papers," she said, "but if he did, it would mean that you were capable of taking care of yourself financially without his help. Now, we would be willing to assist, of course, but you have to prove your ability to be financially independent."

"I virtually am," Eve said. "I made two thousand dollars over the summer and during Christmas vacation waiting tables."

"That's a lot of money."

"Double shifts," Eve said. "My dad was out of work for a long time. After he got another job, he wouldn't let me work anymore after school. But I still have some money left. I dole it out to myself for essentials," she said, half laughing at herself. She was a real miser most of the time.

"Okay. Okay. That's good," Mrs. Decopolis said, thinking. "Why don't you sleep on it. In fact, take a few days and think about it, then let me know. If you want to proceed, I'll draw up the papers.''

"Thanks," Eve said again.

"But Eve," Mrs. Decopolis cautioned, "if you do decide to go ahead, I think you owe it to your father to tell him directly. Not on the phone, but in person."

"Can't you do that?" Eve asked.

"No," Mrs. Decopolis said. "I can't."

"What if I won't see him?" Eve asked.

"I can't force you to. I wouldn't want to do that," Mrs. Decopolis said.

"Will you still handle the paperwork for me?"

"Yes," Mrs. Decopolis said. She walked over to Eve and gave her a hug. But Eve stiffened. She didn't want any hugs. She just wanted out—of everything that made her uncomfortable.

"Wait a minute," Mrs. Decopolis said as they walked into the hallway. She picked up an envelope that was sitting on the hall table. "This is for you," she said, handing the envelope to Eve. "I wanted to give this to you when we had some time to talk about it, but—" She paused and looked directly at Eve. "I told your father if he wrote you a letter explaining some of the things he told me on the phone, you might be able to understand him a little better."

"It's from him?" Eve said, looking at the envelope.

"Yes."

"I don't want it," Eve said, holding it out to Mrs. Decopolis.

"Take it upstairs with you. You might want to read it another time," Mrs. Decopolis said.

"I won't," Eve said.

"Take it upstairs with you anyway," Mrs. Decopolis said.

Eve looked at her for a moment, then she held the letter out in front of her and tore it to shreds.

Chapter Fourteen

She was nervous going up in the elevator. She'd probably get lost and wouldn't find her way around. She hated hospitals. She hated the way they smelled. They were scary. She almost wished she hadn't come. When she got off at the twelfth floor, she looked around for a moment. It looked just like any other hospital ward—a nurses' station, corridors on either side flanked by rooms butting up against each other as if their proximity were some kind of silent protection.

She looked at the piece of paper in her right hand. Room 1206, it said. She slowly headed for the room, the buzzing of the fluorescent light fixtures muddling her brain so that she walked right past it. She turned around and peered into the open doorway.

"Hi," Stephanie said. "Come on in."

She didn't know quite what she had expected. But she hadn't expected what she saw. Stephanie wasn't lying in bed like a revitalized corpse. She looked very much alive and active. Better than she'd looked in a long time.

"Don't be scared," Stephanie said. "It's okay."

"I'm not scared," Eve protested. Even though she was.

Stephanie smiled at her. "We all are sometimes," Stephanie said.

Eve walked into the room and put her canvas bag on the floor next to a chair.

"We can sit in here, or we can go to the dayroom," Stephanie said. "My roommate's there now with her brother."

"We can stay here," Eve said.

"Okay. Why don't you sit down?"

"Yeah," Eve said, trying to settle herself into the hard, blue, nubby chair. They don't make it easy for you, she thought.

"I saw your father that day at school," Stephanie said. Just like that. No preliminaries. No beating around the bush. Eve started to get up from the chair.

"He's an alcoholic, isn't he?" Stephanie asked.

"No. Of course not," Eve said, jumping up. "Listen, I gotta go."

"No, you don't," Stephanie insisted.

"I don't want to talk about my father."

"Okay," Stephanie said. "We'll talk about me, then."

"Okay," Eve said, sitting back down again.

"I'm an alcoholic," Stephanie said.

"Yeah, I know."

"I wish I weren't, but I am."

"I guess that's why you're in here," Eve said. "So you won't be an alcoholic when you get out."

"I'll always be an alcoholic," Stephanie said. "That's one of the things I learned in here."

"Then what good is the program?" Eve asked, shocked.

"The only cure for alcoholism is not to drink," Stephanie said. "Not even one drop. That's why I'll always be an alcoholic, but hopefully I won't be an active one. I'll be what they call here 'a recovering alcoholic.' ''

"Why'd you do it?" Eve asked. "How'd you let yourself get so—"

"So low?" Stephanie laughed.

"Yeah."

"You don't admit your problem till you hit bottom," Stephanie said. "You know the old story as well as I do. I'm not an alcoholic. I only drink beer or wine. Or I don't touch a drop until after six o'clock."

Eve felt uncomfortable, but she brushed the remark aside with a flip retort. "You hit bottom, all right," she said. "And you almost didn't resurface."

"I was already dead before I tried to kill myself," Stephanie said. "Like Carol in *Lemon Sky*. You know where I was sleeping all those nights when I was missing?"

"No," Eve said.

"In some hole along the Venice boardwalk."

"I saw you there once," Eve admitted.

"You probably did. But I didn't see you. Or if I did, it was during a blackout, so I don't remember."

"Oh, come on," Eve said. "You trying to tell me you don't remember some of the things you did?"

"I don't."

"You don't want to."

"That too," Stephanie admitted. "But I do remember a lot of things I'd rather forget, so I know that when people tell me I did certain things during a blackout, I probably did them. I just don't remember."

"I don't know if I buy that one," Eve said.

"I found my older brother," Stephanie said. "Of course, now I can't figure out why the hell I was looking for Peter in the first place. I mean why I was *really* looking for him. Not what I told myself. When Jimmy was arrested, it about drove me crazy. I felt like I had to do all the things Jimmy did to keep him alive. My mom wouldn't let me go to see him. I couldn't stand thinking about him locked up. He can't stand being locked up. I thought I was looking for Peter so he could help me get Jimmy out.''

''What happened when you found Peter?'' Eve asked, though she wasn't sure she really wanted to hear the answer.

''He lives around,'' Stephanie said. ''He lives with a bunch of other people in this filthy place near the board-walk. If you can call it living. You know, the kind of people who don't have faces—the kind you don't want to look in the eyes—'cause you're afraid they'll look back at you.''

''I know,'' Eve said quietly.

''You don't think they'd be people you might recognize. You never think they might be someone in your family. Not *your* family. Your nice middle-class family. *They'd* never panhandle for change for a cheap bottle of booze. They're just people who make you feel guilty for not being able to look at them.''

''You lived with them?''

''My brother came to the hospital after I was admitted here. They dug him out of his hole, and he came here 'cause he said he wanted to help me. He said he started me drinking in the first place.''

''When you stayed with him?''

''I've been drinking for a long, long time,'' Stephanie said. ''You don't become an alcoholic in a week. He's a lot older than I am. By the time I was born, he was already eleven or twelve. He was already a drunk,'' Stephanie said with some bitterness in her voice. ''He used to baby-sit me, and he'd put liquor in my bottle to keep me quiet.'' There was a painful silence in the room. "I've been an alcoholic all my life," Stephanie said finally.

"But nobody knew," Eve protested.

"Not for a long time," Stephanie said. "Not till Jimmy was carted off. Then I wanted people to know, I guess, so I started screwing up."

"What about your mother?"

"She was the last person to admit it," Stephanie said. "It wasn't until Peter told her I'd been sleeping in a coffin in his place."

"You were what?"

"That's one of the things I don't remember," Stephanie said, "but there's no reason for my brother to make it up. He said I slept in a coffin they had stolen for a joke because I thought I was the angel of death."

"Oh, my God." Eve sighed.

"Nobody wants to be an alcoholic, Eve."

"I believe you," Eve said.

"No, you don't."

"I do."

"Maybe you do, but you don't want to admit it," Stephanie said.

"He only drinks when things get tough," Eve shouted.

"Things are always tough. One thing or another."

"You think I should feel sorry for him, don't you?"

"Hell, no. It's time for him to get off the pity pot. Stop feeling sorry for himself. It's time for you to get off the pity pot too. Stop feeling sorry for yourself for having to carry the big burden."

"Yeah, I do," Eve admitted. "I do feel sorry for myself sometimes."

"Maybe what you really feel is scared," Stephanie said quietly. "Maybe that's what he feels too. People drink 'cause they're scared, you know. Not because they want to hurt anybody else."

Eve started to blank out. The ozone layer in the room was getting a little thick. She'd have to leave.

"Thanks for saving my life," Stephanie said quickly. "I never got a chance to thank you. You're a real rescuer whether you want to be or not."

"What do you mean?"

"Nothing," Stephanie said. "Nothing. I hope I can help you out someday, that's all."

"I hope I won't need that kind of help," Eve said, smiling at her.

"Yeah," Stephanie said sadly. "So do I."

"I really do have to go now," Eve said, getting up.

"I'm glad you came," Stephanie said.

"It's probably lonely here," Eve said.

"No. It's not lonely. We're busy all day long. Exercising, therapy, AA meetings."

"AA meetings?"

"Alcoholics Anonymous."

"Oh yeah, Delphi's mom told me about it."

"They get us started right away so it'll be natural for us to keep going when we get out of here."

"I'll see you when you get home," Eve said.

"Next week," Stephanie said.

"What can I do for you in the meantime?"

"Stop being so hard on yourself," Stephanie said, smiling.

"I'm—"

"Yes, you are."

"But—"

"No 'buts.' Give yourself a pat on the back once in awhile. And let someone else give you one too. Nobody can do it by themselves all the time. Nobody."

I can, Eve thought, but she didn't say it out loud.

Eve smiled as she walked to the bus stop. "Give yourself a pat on the back once in a while," she heard

Stephanie say. "And let someone else give you one too. Nobody can do it by themselves all the time." Jargon. Stephanie had wasted her breath on the wrong person.

She hopped on the bus, and her thoughts sped along with it. "Nobody wants to be an alcoholic," she kept hearing over and over again as the traffic whizzed by.

Chapter Fifteen

Eve opened her eyes to a dazzling day. Life could offer so much if you were open to it, she thought as she turned toward Delphi's bed. She was in a very good mood.

"Delphi—you hiding under the covers?" she said, laughing.

Delphi didn't answer.

"Come on," she coaxed. "It's almost ten-thirty."

Still no answer.

"Del," she whispered, getting out of bed. Either Delphi was totally passed out, or she was sick. Eve stood over her bed and pulled back the covers. To her surprise, Delphi was gone. Delphi never got out of bed before she did. Eve usually had to drag her to the bathroom to get her ready for school in the morning. Something must be up, she decided as she padded to the bathroom herself.

The door was wide open. No one was there. "Delphi," she called down the stairs.

"She went to play tennis about an hour ago," her brother Harry yelled.

Delphi—play tennis? The only thing Delphi liked to exercise was her mouth. She'd do an occasional lap or two in the family pool sometimes, but that was only to break in a new bathing suit or cool off if it got too hot lying in the sun.

Eve brushed her teeth and flew downstairs to see what was going on.

"So, what's up?" she asked Harry.

"The Dodgers lost yesterday," he said, studying the sports section of the paper.

"Don't you ever think about anything but sports?" Eve laughed.

"No," he answered without looking up. "What else is there to think about?"

"Music. Movies. Books," Eve said.

"I listen to music," he said. "I read books."

"About sports," she said sarcastically.

"So—what do you read—romances? I read detective stories too," he said defensively.

Eve started to laugh. She was beginning to feel like a member of the family.

"Where's Del?"

"Told you. She's playing tennis. At least she took my mom's racket with her, and she was wearing the skimpiest tennis shorts I've ever seen."

"Really?"

"She'll probably win too. The geek she went with couldn't take his eyes off her legs. He'll probably never even see the damn ball."

"Who was he?"

"Who?"

"The geek—I mean the guy she went with."

"I don't know," Harry said, disgusted. "She didn't bother introducing me."

"What'd he look like?"

"I don't know."

"Was he short, tall, blond—dark?"

"Yeah."

"Yeah, what?"

"Yeah, he was."

"You're impossible."

"I heard her call him Nick. As in Niiiiik, you look sooooo terrific in that shirrrrt."

Eve laughed out loud as she poured herself some juice. "Nick Taylor," she said. "She had a date with Nick Taylor? That jerk. She didn't even tell me."

"She didn't even tell you cause she snuck into the house at two o'clock in the morning," Harry said, "and you were probably sound asleep."

"She was with him last night?"

"Hey, you don't have to be a detective to figure that one out," Harry said. "Or maybe if you read the kind of books I read, you'd be able to figure it out too."

"Okay, smart-ass," Eve said, grabbing the newspaper from Harry. "Tell me how you figured it out."

"Simple," Harry said, grabbing the paper back. "She was in a good mood this morning, so I know she had a good time last night."

"What!"

"And—I was in the den watching a movie on cable. I heard her say, 'See you tomorrow, Niiiiick,' before she closed the front door."

"There you are, Eve," Mrs. Decopolis said, coming into the kitchen.

"Hi, Mrs. Decopolis," Eve said.

"You going to be around today?" Mrs. Decopolis asked.

"Not really," Eve said. "Unless you want me to do something for you. Ah—Torbin is picking me up at noon."

"Ah-ha—Torbin." Mrs. Decopolis laughed. "I guess you still don't consider yourself a member of the family if you said you'd be willing to stay home to help me rather than run off with the man of your dreams."

Eve blushed.

"I'm just kidding," Mrs. Decopolis said. "Go have fun."

"But if I was going to be here," Eve asked, "what would you have wanted me to do? I mean, maybe I can do it when I get back."

"Nothing, really," Mrs. Decopolis said.

"No—tell me," Eve insisted, noticing some papers in Mrs. Decopolis's hand. "Did you want me to take those to the post office for you, or something?"

"Actually," Mrs. Decopolis said. Then she hesitated a moment.

"What?" Eve asked.

"These are the papers," Mrs. Decopolis explained. "I finally had a moment to draw them up. They're ready to be signed by you and by your father."

Eve heaved a sigh. These were the papers she had been waiting for. They were her invitation to freedom. Her own emancipation proclamation. She reached out for them.

"I just thought we ought to talk about it a little," Mrs. Decopolis said. "Before you actually sign them. Before you ask your father to sign them."

"I'm not going to ask him," Eve said. "I'm just going to send them to him with a note. That's what I decided to do."

"Okay." Mrs. Decopolis sighed. She handed Eve the papers. "Just do me one favor. Don't sign them until you've read them carefully. I want you to know exactly what it is you're signing. If you have any questions at all, please, please ask me. Okay?"

"Okay," Eve promised.

"So, where are you going with Torbin?" Mrs. Decopolis asked.

"To the mountains," Eve said happily. "On a picnic."

"You want Sophia to pack you some sandwiches?"

"No thanks, Torbin said we'd stop on the way," Eve explained.

"You've been seeing a lot of him, haven't you?" Mrs. Decopolis asked.

"Do you mind?" Eve asked, worried.

"Of course not," Mrs. Decopolis said. "He seems like a very nice guy."

Eve smiled; why did parents always think saying someone was a very nice guy was a compliment? Sure, he was a nice guy, but that was so bland. Who couldn't be a nice guy? He was much more than that. He was— wonderful.

"I better get ready," she yelled, running out of the kitchen with the papers.

"What about breakfast?" Mrs. Decopolis called after her.

"I had breakfast," Eve called back.

"A glass of orange juice," Mrs. Decopolis said under her breath.

Eve laughed. Nobody had ever worried about her eating breakfast before.

She was standing at the window when Torbin pulled up. She was about to step back out of the way so he wouldn't see her. She didn't want him to know how anxious she was to see him. But she didn't move in time, and he waved to her and smiled before he got out of the car.

Every time she saw him it felt like the first time. Each time she was excited, almost breathless, waiting for him to walk the short distance from the car to the front door. She could feel his electricity right through the walls.

"Ready?" he asked, taking her hand.

"For you," Eve said.

He smiled at her. She was being flirtatious, and it was fun.

They drove up into the mountains to a spot Torbin knew, way up high, about an hour from town. It was so quiet, so far away from what people called civilization. They were entirely alone, but they weren't the least bit lonely. They filled the whole mountainside with the sounds of their whispered voices, which echoed through the crevices, bounced off the rocks, and boomeranged back to them like the caresses of a summer wind.

Though it was very warm at the bottom of the mountain, it was at least fifteen degrees cooler where they were sitting. It was actually a little chilly. Eve was glad Torbin had warned her to bring along a jacket.

He wouldn't let her do a thing. He set out their picnic on a flat rock. He even brought a blanket to put under it. What could be better? she wondered. Chicken sandwiches, chips, fruit, a couple of soft drinks, and the person she wanted most to be with in the world.

"I like it here," she said, smiling at him.

"I'm glad," he said. "I come here a lot, but I've never brought anyone with me before, except my dad."

"Your dad?" Eve laughed. "That must be romantic."

"Hey," Torbin said, giving her a friendly punch on the arm, "you don't know my dad."

"Hey"—she laughed—"you're right."

"So—I'll introduce you sometime. If and when I'm sure you can behave properly in adult company," he teased.

"I behave in adult company," she teased back. "I know how to act with you, don't I?"

"That's putting it mildly," he said, laughing. "I only

wish you didn't know how to act. I would sure love to show you.''

''Meaning what, pea brain?'' she said, taking a bite of her sandwich.

''Meaning here we are alone on a mountaintop, and 'I vant to suck your blood,' '' he said, imitating Dracula.

''I knew there was something different about you,'' she said. ''But why are you out in broad daylight, Count?''

''I confess I am not a true vampire,'' Torbin said with a heavy Hungarian accent, or at least what he thought was a heavy Hungarian accent.

''A phony? You're just another phony like the rest of us?'' Eve said, laughing.

''Yeah, I guess,'' he said. ''I'm just another blood-sucking phony.''

They both laughed and joked around and teased each other, then Torbin picked up the empty paper plates and stashed them in a garbage bag. He picked up the blanket and put it on the flat rock so they would be more comfortable.

''I really would like you to meet my dad,'' he said after they settled down again.

''Sure,'' Eve said, thrilled that he wanted her to meet his father. It might be a little scary, but it meant something, that he wanted her to meet him.

''And I'd like to meet yours too,'' he said innocently.

Eve froze. Her smile and all the laughter inside her body drained out of her as if someone had punched a hole in her smiley-face balloon.

She turned away from Torbin.

''Don't,'' he said. He reached out to touch her, but she shrugged him off.

''Don't,'' she said.

''Eve—''

"Why did you have to spoil everything?" she asked.

"I'm sorry," he said. "I didn't mean to spoil anything. I only meant to—to show you that I love you."

She turned to look at him. Had she heard him right? "What?"

"I love you," he said, "and it hurts me to see you so closed off."

"I don't know what you're talking about," she answered. She was so confused. Why was the balloon soaring one minute and falling to the ground the next? She had never felt so high in her life. She didn't think anyone had ever said that to her before—I love you. No one. Not even her parents, though she knew they did. At least, they must have.

"If you love me," she said slowly, "then don't talk about my father, okay?"

"But I want to talk about it," he said. "It's too important not to talk about."

"Why?"

"Because if you shut off those feelings," he said softly, "you shut off your other feelings too. You have to. You can't turn off an engine partway. It might coast for awhile, but eventually it just eases to a stop one day when you're not even looking, and before you know it, you've rolled so far down the hill, you can't get back up again."

"My engine's running fine," she protested. "And I do have feelings." She hesitated. She wanted to tell him what those feelings were. She wanted to say that she loved him so much that that was all she could feel. That her loving him had given her the courage to let go of her father. She wanted to crawl over next to him, right up against him and cuddle in his arms. She knew she would feel warm and protected. But she didn't say anything, and she didn't do anything. She was too scared. She knew damn well what happened when she loved and trusted people. They disappeared or they disappointed.

Torbin laughed. Not what she would have expected him to do. "Yeah," he said finally. "That's exactly what I used to say."

"You?"

"Don't you want to know why I come up here with my father?" he asked.

"I just thought—"

"We come up here to talk to each other," he explained. "To say all the things we wished we'd said before it was too late."

Chapter Sixteen

"She wanted so much," Torbin said quietly. "She wanted to be the best mother, the best wife, the best doctor—"

"She was a doctor?" Eve asked, surprised.

"Yeah," Torbin said. "She and my dad met in medical school. They were the perfect couple. They got married. Had the perfect wedding. Bought the perfect house. Had the perfect kid."

"She had everything," Eve said.

"That's what my dad said."

"Then why?"

"That's what I asked."

"Did you find the answer?"

"Sort of." Torbin sighed. "Only I wish I'd have found it a lot sooner than I did. My dad and I both do. I don't know. Maybe it wouldn't have mattered to her. Maybe things would have ended exactly the same way. But it would have mattered to us."

"When did she start drinking?" Eve asked.

"I don't know," Torbin said. "I just always remember seeing her with a drink when she got home from the office. She used to say it was her calming-down time. She'd pour us both an orange juice. Only she'd add a little something to hers. A little vodka. A little gin.''

"I know all about that," Eve said. "Calming-down times which turn into time out entirely. Time out of the world.''

" 'Cause you're passed out," Torbin said.

"Yeah, 'cause you're passed out.''

"It happened gradually," Torbin said. "We didn't even notice. I guess she didn't either. One day when I was about ten I realized the calming-down time lasted a whole lot longer. And the next day I realized she had already begun calming down before she came home.''

"At her office?" Eve asked, shocked.

"That's what made my dad crazy," Torbin said. "I used to hear them arguing about it. 'You can't do that to your patients,' he'd say. 'You're a doctor, for God's sake. You took an oath. You're taking people's lives in your hands, and you can't even keep your hands from shaking.' Then he'd tell her she was a loser. A real loser.''

"How could she do that?" Eve asked. "That's so terrible.''

"She couldn't help it," Torbin said. "She was an alcoholic. She knew she was. She'd lay off for a month of two—then she'd be really unbearable to live with.'' He laughed. "It was worse than when she was drinking.''

"My mother used to yell at my father, 'You're nasty when you're not drinking. You're no fun at all. Go get some booze so we can have a good time.' ''

"So your mother allowed your father to drink. Even if she didn't know it, she probably wanted him to. It's hard to be a dry drunk. Someone who stops cold turkey without the support of some kind of program. It's hard enough with a program, I guess." He paused and looked directly at Eve. "Was your mother an alcoholic too?"

Eve didn't want to answer that question. She'd pushed it so far back in her mind that it had disappeared entirely. She knew, of course, what the answer was. She had known for a long time, but it wasn't the kind of thing she wanted to think about. It wouldn't exactly light up her life everyday. And more than that, it complicated things. If her mother was an alcoholic, too, then her father wasn't solely responsible for her misery, and for her mother's walking out on them.

"Yes," she heard herself say, almost as if someone else were saying it, "I guess my mother must have been an alcoholic."

Of course as soon as she said it she realized that she had fallen into a trap. She had admitted that both her parents were alcoholics. A few months ago she couldn't even admit that her father was.

"Sometimes I think that's better," Torbin said.

"How could it be better?" Eve asked.

"Then at least the person who's an alcoholic has someone else to—I don't know—identify with, maybe."

"Get drunk with, you mean," Eve said sarcastically.

"Hey, there's nothing sadder than a woman—or a man—who's reeling around out there all by himself."

"Like your mother?"

"My father used to have a drink or two with her, but never more than that. When he realized how much she was drinking, he wouldn't understand why she couldn't control herself. After all, she wasn't some ignorant ditch digger who didn't know how to spell her own name, he'd say. She was a brilliant doctor."

"Look," Eve said. "I don't mean to be rude, but I really can't understand why she couldn't control it either, if she was so smart."

"That's why I was so angry with her," Torbin said. "That and the fact that she left. I could never forgive her for leaving until after she died. I finally realized that she'd left as much for me as anything. She didn't want to embarrass me—us—my dad and me."

"Why didn't she just dry up?" Eve asked. "You have money. She could have gone into some program or something. The Betty Ford Clinic in Palm Springs. Half the celebrities in California have gone through the detox program there."

"She was too embarrassed, I think," Torbin said. "Control was this major issue in our house. I mean, I heard it a lot. 'Control yourself.' 'Control your temper, young man.' 'We have to take control of the situation before it gets out of hand.' You know, stuff like that. I think when she realized she couldn't control her drinking, it was easier for her to leave than for her to admit she needed help."

"What about her medical practice?"

"Oh yes, her medical practice," Torbin said, his jaws clenched. "She was asked to leave the medical association. She made too many diagnostic mistakes. No one died from them. No one even suffered much, but near the end the other doctors were tired of covering for her, and there were too many days when she just couldn't make it to the office."

"So they gave her the boot?"

"That and a few other unpleasant words of wisdom," Torbin said. "But it was better than what my dad and I gave her, I guess."

"What did you give her?"

"Nothing," Torbin said. "Nothing that would help her, anyway. My dad said she deserved it."

"That's pretty heavy," Eve said. "Under the best of circumstances that's hard for anyone to hear."

"And me—" He paused and sighed, as if it were just

too painful for him to remember. "Me," he went on finally. "I walked away from her when she fell into the living room and lay on the floor calling for help."

"But what could you do?" Eve said, feeling his pain, wanting to take it away. Wanting to make him feel better. Wanting to help him forget about it. Hoping he'd stop talking. Knowing he had to say it, and she'd have to listen. Wondering how much more she could bear to hear without zoning out herself.

"If I'd have known what I know now," he said, "I'd have stood by her at least. I'd have offered to help. I'd have gone to some kind of program with her so she wouldn't have felt so alone."

"And what if she wouldn't have gone?"

"Maybe she wouldn't have," he said. "And if she hadn't, I could have let go. I'd have known I did what I could have done."

"Torbin!" Eve yelled. "You said you were only ten years old."

"A ten-year-old is a man when his mother's a drunk." Torbin sighed.

Without thinking, Eve reached across the blanket for Torbin. She put her arms around him and held him close to her, stroking his back, kissing his hair. She wanted the energy of the love she felt for him to flow into his body from hers. She wanted it to heal his pain, but she knew no matter how much she loved him, or how much he loved her, there was only so much she could do. In the end he had to forgive himself. Heal his own pain.

"You couldn't have done it for her," she said to Torbin. "You could have made it easier, maybe, but she made her own choices."

"Yeah," Torbin whispered, his face against hers. "I'm finally beginning to believe that."

"You could have chosen to be bitter and closed off,"

she said, "but you didn't. You chose to be what you are."

"And what's that?" he asked, rolling down the blanket with her.

"If you're fishing for compliments, I'll give them to you," she said, smiling at him. "You're the most honest, thoughtful, kindest—and funniest person I've ever met," she said. "And some other stuff too, but I wouldn't want you to think you're that terrific. You might decide to turn me in for a better model."

"No chance," he said, kissing her. "I really do love you."

"I love you too," she said, and she was surprised at how natural it sounded. It sounded as if she had said it a million times before.

"More than Tom Cruise?" he teased.

"Ya know," she said. "Sometimes reproductions are even better than originals."

He laughed.

"And other times," she continued, "when you really look at what you thought was a reproduction, you realize how wrong you were. That it wasn't a reproduction, after all. In fact you can't even remember why you saw any similarity in the first place because what you have in front of you now is the most original piece of work in the world."

"Aw, you're just saying that 'cause it's true," he said, laughing.

"You're blushing," she said.

"Big boys blush," he teased.

"Now you're making another wise-ass remark."

"Hey, when did you get to be so honest all of a sudden?"

"Oh—about five minutes ago," she said.

Chapter Seventeen

"Stephanie!" Eve cried when she opened the door. "You're out of the hospital."

"I'm home," Stephanie said.

"Come on in. Can you?" Eve asked as she ushered Stephanie into the hallway.

"Actually," Stephanie said, resisting the temptation to let herself be swept into the house, "I came to ask you for a favor."

"Sure," Eve said. "Anything. You look terrific. Great. You really do."

"Yeah," Stephanie said. "And I want to keep it this way too."

"So, what can I do for you?"

"Take a ride with me."

"A ride—that's it?"

"Well, not exactly," Stephanie said. "I—I just need a little moral support."

"You got it," Eve said, grabbing her canvas bag from the stairway. "Where are we going?"

"Broadway and Tenth," Stephanie said.

Eve stopped walking. Broadway and Tenth was her

old neighborhood. It reminded her that there was a legal document upstairs in her room waiting to be signed, waiting for her to send a copy to her father. Maybe she'd run up and get it, stick it into his mailbox as long as she was in the area. On the other hand, why ask for trouble? What if he was home?

"What are you looking for in that neighborhood?" she asked as they got into Stephanie's car.

"Moral support."

"I thought that's what you wanted from me." Eve laughed.

"I do," Stephanie said. "I need your moral support to get me to where I have to go to get the moral support I need."

"Okay," Eve said. "You lost me, but if you want to run that past me again, maybe I can follow you this time."

"When I was at the hospital, they took all the kids in the program to this teen drop-in center and said it would be a good idea to spend some time hanging around there after we got out."

"Hey, I'm sure there's a drop-in center closer to your neighborhood," Eve suggested.

"Not for recovering alcoholics," Stephanie said.

"You mean you're going to hang out with a bunch of drunks?" Eve asked, amazed. Of course, the minute it was out of her mouth, she was sorry. She saw Stephanie cringe. She wasn't usually so insensitive, but for some strange reason she almost wanted to hurt Stephanie, and for the life of her she couldn't figure out why.

"Recovering drunks," Stephanie said, trying to smile. "The theory is that we all help each other stay sober. People who don't have the same problem get pretty bored listening to us all the time."

Eve started to protest.

"No. No. It's true," Stephanie said. "There are

times we have trouble getting through the day without—
without a bottle—you know? Other recovering alcoholics don't mind those calls for help in the middle of the
night. They've made the same kinds of calls themselves.''

"I'm sorry, Stephanie," Eve said. "I guess I just feel
a little nervous about going there."

"Hey, how the hell do you think I feel?" Stephanie
asked. "That's why I roped you into going along."

Why me? Eve wanted to ask. But she couldn't.

They drove the rest of the way without talking. Music
blared from the radio much louder than usual, giving
Eve a headache, and Stephanie smoked one cigarette
after another, causing Eve's eyes to burn in spite of the
fact that both windows were wide open.

Eve coughed.

"Sorry," Stephanie said, putting out the cigarette.
"Bad habit. But it's a better one than drinking." She
laughed. "Boy, get into a room with recovering alcoholics and you can't see across it to the other side. You
think the smog in L.A. is bad. It's nothing compared
with the smoke screen recovering alcoholics put between themselves and the rest of the world."

"I guess smoking's an addiction too," Eve said.

"Yeah," Stephanie admitted. "We all know that, but
when you give up the one thing that was the center of
your life, you have to substitute something else. Some
people go for candy and sweet stuff, but a lot of us go
for this kind of oral gratification. My mom says when
she was younger, people called cigarettes coffin nails."

"Coffin nails." Eve laughed. "It's pretty hard to pick
up a cigarette if you call it that."

"Not if you're still unsure about whether you want
to live or die," Stephanie said.

Eve bit her lip and glanced over at Stephanie.

"Oh, don't worry. I didn't mean it literally," Stephanie assured her. "I'm not going to pull that one again. I just meant that going through a twenty-one- or twenty-eight-day program helps you get your head straight, but there are no guarantees that life won't go on being painful."

They pulled up in front of a rundown building, the kind that seemed to mushroom out of no place when no one was looking. Someone had painted the building a vivid blue, and there was a rainbow on top of the doorway.

"This is it," Stephanie said, opening the car door.

"Doesn't look so bad," Eve said, looking at a sign taped to the window of the door to the building. AB-SOLUTELY NO ONE OVER 19 ADMITTED. Then who the hell runs the place? Eve wondered. A bunch of toddlers?

Eve walked in after Stephanie. She looked around the room crowded with mismatched, dilapidated furniture. This was no drop-in center. This was a center for rejects from the Venice boardwalk. These were the people she tried to avoid seeing. They scared her. Not that she didn't see them around her old neighborhood all the time, but seeing them and socializing with them wasn't exactly the same thing. She wanted to run back to the car and lock herself in. She wondered if Stephanie's reaction was the same as hers, but before she had a chance to nudge her, a tall, blond girl, slightly overweight but still very all-American looking, very fresh and young and really quite pretty, wandered over to them and introduced herself.

"You working off-hours, or did you just get out of a program?" she asked.

"How'd you know?" Stephanie asked her, without answering her question.

"The eyes," she said. "Give it away every time."

"I don't understand," Stephanie said.

"You will," the girl said. "I'm Rhonda. Welcome to the club. We are definitely exclusive, but as you see"— she swept her hand to take in the rest of the room— "we're not all that particular. As long as you follow the rules, you'll always be welcome."

"Doesn't sound like much of a welcome to me," Stephanie said.

"Hey," Rhonda shot back. "Get off the pity pot. What did you want, a five-piece band?"

"It isn't so easy coming here, you know?"

"It's a lot easier than not coming," Rhonda said. "Follow me. I'll introduce you to the other kids. Bring your friend too," she added, nodding her head at Eve. "They won't bite—unless, of course, you bite them first."

Eve attached herself to Stephanie's side, but after standing around for twenty minutes while Stephanie and four other kids exchanged stories about their various programs, she got bored and wandered off. The place itself felt almost comfortable after awhile, and her heart stopped pounding long enough for her to realize that these kids weren't any different from any other kids. They might look a bit scruffier. From what she could gather, most of them hadn't come out of eight-thousand-dollar rehab programs; they'd crawled in off the street.

Eve wandered around the room, which contained a couch and a few chairs surrounding a large-screen TV, all of which had been donated, according to Rhonda. Six guys around fifteen or sixteen were sitting in front of the TV watching a video tape of some Stallone film, which seemed a bit ironic to Eve. But people get their heroes where they can find them, she guessed.

All six guys were so intently glued to the screen, Godzilla could have walked into the room, and they wouldn't have noticed.

However, in a second room adjoining the first, there was an electric tension in the air. A pool table dominated the area, and the competition both for its use and for the game itself was intense. These guys were all there, one hundred percent alert. Even though none of them actually took their eyes from the pool table, she knew they all saw her. Every detail. She felt as if she had been stripped to her essence, and that they knew, without any exchange of words, that she didn't belong.

She turned and peeked around a makeshift partition in back of which were squeezed two old oak desks. Each desk was stacked high with papers, cans of soda, and a phone. Behind the desks were posters. They were funny. They were also meant as a signal to anyone who looked at them that it was okay to laugh at yourself sometimes. On one poster was a porpoise wearing sunglasses. Another showed a monkey leaning against a brick wall. Under the wall, in bold red letters, were the words "Just when I know all of life's answers, they change the questions."

"Is there anything I can do to help you?" Eve heard.

She looked down. Sitting at one of the old desks was a large, cherubic-faced woman who, despite her size, just seemed to melt into the area as if she were part of the furniture. This was her space. She belonged here.

"No," Eve said, though if she ever did need help, this woman looked as if she'd already shouldered half the problems of the world and might be pretty good at finding a spot on her back for one more.

"Well, how about helping me, then?" the woman said. "I'm Anne Ronelli, and you are . . . ?"

"Oh, I'm just here with a friend," Eve explained. "I don't belong here."

"Well, you still have a name, don't you? Even if you're just here with a friend," Anne said, smiling at Eve so openly and so warmly that it made her heart hurt for the woman. No one could afford to be that open in this life.

"I'm Eve Morrison."

"Well, Eve Morrison." Anne laughed as she hauled herself off the chair. "I repeat my question. How about helping me?"

"I guess," Eve said, not really wanting to commit herself before she knew what it was this woman wanted from her.

"Come on. Come on," Anne said, picking up her can of diet iced tea and striding out of her area to a makeshift kitchen off the pool room. She was amazingly light on her feet for so large a woman.

Anne began unloading loaves of bread on the counter. "Line them up," she said to Eve. "I'll get the peanut butter, and we'll have these made in no time."

As Anne reached into a cupboard for the peanut butter, a girl about Eve's age ran over to her and gave her a hug. "I did it, Mom. I did it."

"Knew you could," Anne said.

"Not without your help," the girl said.

"I just made the call," Anne said. "You did the rest yourself."

"I start tomorrow," the girl said. "They're training me in the morning, and I can bus tables in the afternoon. If I'm good at it and they see that I'm serious, I can train to be a waitress next month when they have an opening."

"That's wonderful, darling," Anne said.

"I'm going to tell Rhonda," the girl said, hugging Anne again. "I'm so excited. I can't believe it."

"That your daughter?" Eve asked as she spread some peanut butter on the bread laid out in front of her, which, like the furniture, was also donated, she learned.

"Nah." Anne laughed.

"But she called you Mom," Eve said, confused.

"They all call me Mom after they get to know me," Anne said.

Eve glanced over at several black guys surrounding the pool table to their left.

"Them, too." Anne laughed again. "We're color-blind around here."

Eve laughed with her. She liked this woman.

"Yeah, some of these kids haven't seen their biological mothers for years," Anne said, pouring various cans of soup into a big pot.

Eve felt that familiar lump of recognition begin to expand in her throat.

"So how's your relationship with your parents?" Anne asked casually as she ran a wooden spoon around the big pot.

Eve shrugged her shoulders. She didn't trust herself to speak.

"Not very good, huh?" Anne said.

Eve ran her fingers through her hair and looked down at the bread.

"Hey, Mom," a boy yelled as he bounded into the room.

Eve put the knife down. This was her chance to escape.

"I got the contract," he said as Eve slipped out of the kitchen area. "I'm going to sing backup on a record. A real record that will be sold in real stores," he yelled. Then he jumped up and down, hugging Anne and kissing her.

Eve found Stephanie and tugged on her arm. "I gotta go," she said quietly.

"Ten minutes," Stephanie said, interrupting an intense conversation.

"Listen," Eve said, "this is my old neighborhood. I have some things to do around here. I'll find my own way back to Delphi's."

"You sure?" Stephanie asked.

"Yeah," Eve said, "I'm sure."

"Okay, so we'll see you," Rhonda said.

"I don't think so," Eve said, "but it was nice meeting you."

"I doubt it." Rhonda laughed. "But it was probably nice meeting Mom. She's the best. Trust me. You can trust her."

"I'm not a recovering alcoholic," Eve insisted. "I just came along with Stephanie."

"We have Al-Anon meetings here too," Rhonda said. "For families of alcoholics. Every Saturday at twelve-thirty." She checked her watch. "Five minutes. Stick around. You might find it interesting."

"No, thanks," Eve said, holding her canvas bag to her and sidling toward the front door.

"She knows how come you're here," Rhonda said, putting her arm across the doorway. "We all know."

"I'm here 'cause Stephanie asked me to do her a favor," Eve said angrily.

"It's in the eyes," Rhonda said. "You can always see it in the eyes. You got the body of a sixteen-year-old, the face of a sixteen-year-old, and the eyes of a sixty-year-old."

Eve shoved Rhonda's arm out of the way and burst through the door.

Once outside, she ran for two blocks until she was out of breath. It felt better just getting away from that place. The smoke was disgusting. It had filled every pore of her body. She felt it emanating from her hair and her clothes. She wished she could jump into a shower and wash it all off along with everything else in her life she didn't want to face.

I'm going to do it, she said to herself. I'm going to talk to him face to face. I'm not a coward. I can't just send him the legal papers with a note.

She crossed the street to a phone booth, but the phone was out of order.

I'll just walk over there, she decided. If he's home, he's home. If not, it wasn't meant to be.

Chapter Eighteen

His truck was in the driveway. She could see it when she rounded the corner. Her heart started to beat wildly, and she took a deep breath to calm herself down. Why was she so nervous? What could he possibly say or do at this point that could persuade her to change her mind? She didn't care if he had been sober for a month. What's a month? She didn't even care that he had another job. He'd probably lose that one too. Still, he was her father. She did have some feelings for him, and they weren't all negative.

As long as he left her alone they could be civil to each other. She wouldn't even mind seeing him once in awhile. She'd even *like* to see him once in awhile. As she started to walk up the front path, her heart began to race faster and faster. She wanted to run the rest of the way to catch up with it. She missed him. She missed him much more than she could afford to admit to herself.

She scrounged around in her canvas bag for her house keys, which she still kept with her for old times' sake. She found them and was about to unlock the door, but decided to knock instead. This wasn't really her house anymore. It didn't seem right to just walk in unexpectedly.

She knocked lightly, but no one answered. She knocked again, harder this time. Still no answer. Maybe he had walked down to the store.

She was about to sit down on the front stoop to wait for him when she heard the door open. She turned around. He was standing there, his shirt hanging out from his wrinkled trousers, his hair in spikes all over his head, as if some hairdresser with a bizarre sense of humor had covered it with mousse and blow-dried it in every direction. He obviously hadn't shaved in days.

"I—it's you," he stammered, trying to tuck his shirt into his trousers.

She didn't say anything. She just stared at him.

"Been working hard," he said. "Just got up."

"Yeah, I see," Eve said, disgusted with him and with herself for thinking it could ever be any different.

He put his hands over his eyes to shield them from the light. "You've been gone a long time," he said.

"Not long enough," she answered back.

Her father tried to pull himself together. He half smiled at her in a strange, eerie way. "You look good—better than ever. Like a kid again."

"What do you mean?" Eve asked, her stomach turning around and around, zooming up to her throat. Somehow she knew what he meant, but she couldn't believe it.

"Guess the world out there's not so terrific, after all," he said with a catch in his voice.

"Stop it," Eve cried, her hands over her ears. "Stop talking like that."

"I said I'd never let you in the house again," he stammered, "but the door's open. If you want to come in, come in."

He made a grandiose gesture as if to sweep away any cobwebs of pain that might prevent her from entering the house.

"I'm going," Eve said, and she turned to walk away.

"Don't," he pleaded as two people walked by and stopped to see what was going on.

"Stop it," Eve yelled. "I told you to stop it."

"You left just like that. Without even saying goodbye to Eve. Now she's gone too," he mumbled.

Eve saw his eyes fill up with tears.

"Get in the house," Eve commanded as she pushed him inside the door.

He stumbled into the dark living room and tripped on an empty beer can.

Eve picked it up, then flung it back down on the floor again.

"I'm sorry, baby," he said, reaching out for her. "I'm really, really sorry."

"Shut up," Eve cried, suddenly frightened. A horrible wave of nausea was working its way through her stomach. "Just shut up."

"Come home, Kaya," he said, but his words were so slurred, they sounded like slush coming out of his mouth.

"I'm Eve—not Mom," Eve screamed at him. "Listen to me." But she knew he was lost in his own fog and hadn't heard a word she had said. "I don't know why I even bother talking to you when you're like this. You'll never remember anything I say, anyway. But I'm still going to say it, and if you don't remember, that's your tough luck." Her words came out in a rush. "I came here to talk to you, to tell you that I—that I don't want to live like this, without the two of us speaking. You have a problem. Okay, I know that now, and I don't want to hold it against you. But unless you do something about it—something—I can't stand to be around you. Do you understand? I want to see you, be with you, but not when you're like *this*."

Her throat was so tight she couldn't say anything else. If only she could cry, she'd feel better. But look at him, standing there slobbering. He was disgusting. He turned her stomach. She couldn't stand to see such weakness.

She was going to walk out of this house and never come back here again. She'd send him the papers. She didn't care how he reacted to them as long as he signed them.

She kicked another beer can out of the way and walked to the door, but she couldn't walk through it without offering him a hand. She didn't want to spend the rest of her life like Torbin, feeling guilty for not making one last try. She didn't want to go to his funeral, thinking it might be different if only—

"You're an alcoholic," she said. "You can get help if you really want to."

He reached out for her.

"Don't," she said automatically. Then she was sorry she had recoiled from him. She could see the look of hurt travel over his face and slip into his neck as he bowed his head to his chest.

"I know a place," she said. "I could find out where to go. I'll go with you."

"Stay with me," he pleaded. "I'm so lonely."

"No," she said. "I can't do that, but if you'll go to one AA meeting yourself, I'll go to the next one with you."

"Kaya," he cried as he grabbed her tightly and began kissing and touching her.

"No!" Eve screamed. "Get away from me. I hate you. Get away from me."

He backed her against the wall, and she lashed out at him, slicing his cheek with her fingernails.

He looked at her with hatred for a moment. Then he suddenly recognized who she was.

The blood drained from his face as he put his hand over his mouth in horror. "My God, what have I done? Oh, my God," he said over and over again as Eve stood there panting with hatred and fear.

"I could kill myself. I swear to God, Eve, I could kill myself."

"Go ahead," she said. "Finish the job."

"Eve," he wailed.

"I'm never coming back here," she screamed. "Never. Never. Never. And this time I mean it."

"I don't blame you," he said, sinking to the floor.

"Remember that. Remember that tomorrow when you wake up from all the booze you're going to consume as soon as I walk out of here. Remember that when you wake up stinking from your own vomit. I'm never coming back."

Chapter Nineteen

Eve ran, stumbling over her emotions, as she fled from her father. Though she was hot from running, she shivered. She didn't know where she was going—only that she had to get there. She couldn't forget the look on her father's face. The feel of his hands when he touched her. No matter how hard she ran, they were with her. Her heart beat so fast she felt as if it would explode into a thousand pieces.

She found herself standing in front of the phone booth outside the teen drop-in center. She put in some change and began to dial Torbin's number, but her mind went blank, and she couldn't remember it. Still panting, she dumped everything from her canvas bag all over the sidewalk and searched through the mess, barely conscious of exactly what she was looking for. She only knew that she would find it in the bag.

She threw her hairbrush back in. She tossed her math book and her pens and pencils back. She picked up her wallet, a scarf, a toothbrush, toothpaste, underwear, shampoo, a T-shirt, two tapes, and a smooth stone she had picked up the day she and Torbin had hiked up the mountain. She threw her juggling balls back in. Then she found it. Torbin's phone number, scratched on a piece of paper. "Call me if you need anything," he had said to her at the bus stop.

Her hands were shaking, but she dialed. The ringing pierced her ears, jangling her nerves like an electrical jolt. It rang and rang, but no one answered.

Stunned, she let the phone slip from her hands and dangle on the gray wire, still ringing. People were never there when you needed them. Never. And what would she have said to him anyway? She couldn't talk about what had happened. She didn't even want to think about it. But she couldn't think about anything else. She had somehow forgotten how to zone out.

The raucous sounds of heavy-metal music and loud voices broke her trance. Anne was locking up the teen center, and a bunch of kids were vying for her attention, for one last word of assurance before they were on their way for the rest of the weekend.

Anne turned around, and her eyes met Eve's. "Okay, kids, get lost," she said. "See you on Tuesday. Have peace, have fun, and let the sun shine in."

The sad-eyed kids went away grumbling. It was as if they were being evicted from the only home they knew, the only stability in their lives. Some of them gave Anne a kiss or a hug. Others sauntered off, angry with the parent surrogate they called Mom. Angry because they had no place else to go, but even she couldn't break the rules and let them spend the weekend at the center.

Even after they had all rounded the corner and disappeared, Eve and Anne continued to stare at each other. Eve wanted to sink into Anne's big arms, curl up in her lap while she rocked her to sleep, but she was afraid if she slept she might dream, and she knew what her dreams would be. She knew she would have to face the nightmare if she ever wanted to sleep again.

"My father is an alcoholic," Eve blurted out. That wasn't exactly what she wanted to say, but her brain and her mouth weren't functioning together any longer.

"I forgot something inside," Anne said as she put her arm around Eve and guided her over to the door, holding Eve next to her by the sheer force of her energy as she unlocked the door and pulled her in.

As Eve sank into Anne's huge, tattered, brown leather desk chair, she felt as if she were shrinking. She felt as if she were Alice running after the white rabbit, looking for the key. She felt as if she had fallen through a long, dark tunnel. She wondered if she'd ever get out again, or if she'd be stuck there for the rest of her life, reliving the look on her father's face over and over again.

When she finished telling Anne all the things she never thought she'd be able to tell anyone, she could barely talk. Her throat was dry and constricted. Anne passed Eve her diet iced tea, and Eve sipped on it, but she couldn't even feel it going down her throat.

She was sitting there waiting. Waiting for the fog to roll in and cover her, waiting for the white rabbit to lead her further into the tunnel, to oblivion. She wanted to ask the white rabbit for one little pill that would take it all away. All the pain and hurt that had accumulated in her heart for the past sixteen years.

"Listen to me, Eve," Anne said gently. "Don't be frightened and don't feel guilty about what I'm going to say."

"I know. I know," Eve said, barely above a whisper. But she didn't know. She thought Anne was going to tell her it wasn't her fault again. She thought Anne was going to tell her to let go—of her guilt, of her pride, of her father. "Let go and let God" is what she had heard Anne say to one of the other kids.

"I'm going to have to report this," Anne said finally.

It didn't sink in at first. Report it to whom?

Anne picked up the paper on which she had scribbled Eve's last name and phone number and her father's name.

"I'm going to have to call the child protection agency."

"But I'm not a child," Eve blurted out.

"Yes, I know," Anne said. "But you should be. You would be if thieves hadn't stolen your childhood away from you."

"You can't call anybody!"

"I have to. It's the law."

"No."

"Eve, I can't break the law. If anyone found out, they'd shut me down, and I can't afford to place this center in jeopardy."

"What about me?" Eve cried.

"I can't afford to place you in any further jeopardy either," Anne said, emphatically but kindly, very kindly, her dark brown eyes swimming with tears.

Eve was glad someone could cry. She was too scared. And too guilty.

"What will they do to him?"

"The police will probably question him—"

"No!"

"There will be a preliminary hearing before a judge—"

"No! You can't do this to me."

"I'm not doing it to you," Anne said.

"I can't turn in my own father."

"You're not. I am."

"It's sick," Eve said. "Sick to turn in your own father. It's like those kids who turned in their parents for doing cocaine. It's like the Nazis turning in their parents if they suspected they disapproved of the state."

Anne picked up the phone and began to dial.

Eve leaped up from the chair and tried to grab the paper with her vital statistics on it, but Anne pulled it away from her.

"He didn't mean it," Eve cried, trying to reach for the paper.

"There was intent to commit a crime," Anne said.

"He thought I was my mother."

"The judge will have to decide that. I'm not equipped to make those decisions."

Eve started to run for the door. "I can't take this. This is crazy. Nobody told me it would be like this."

"You can't run away from it. Even if you go out that door, I'm still going to place the call," Anne said. "So you might as well come back here so we can talk this out."

Eve stopped, her back to Anne. "I trusted you."

"I'm glad," Anne said.

"I trusted you!"

"Continue to trust me. Your father is a sick man. He needs help, and this is the only way he's going to get it. He tried to—"

Eve put her hands over her ears, but she couldn't block out Anne's words.

"It happened. I can't do anything to change that, and neither can you, but we can deal with it. We can face it together, and we can help your father face it."

Eve was swimming in every emotion she had ever experienced. Anger at Anne, at her father, at Torbin for not being home, at herself. Guilt. Hatred. Fear. Revulsion. Love. That was there too, struggling to get out, trying to work its way up through her stomach, but it was there, even though she couldn't recognize it yet.

"You make your call first," Anne said, handing Eve the phone.

"Who should I call?"

"Your best friend."

"Why?"

"For support. It ain't going to be easy getting through this."

"I don't have any friends."

"Trust me."

Eve took the phone from Anne's hand and dialed Torbin's number again. This time he answered.

"My father—" she began, then all the tears that had been stored in the pit of her stomach came rushing out in a torrent, flooding the phone, the desk, her face, and her clothes. She had been caught in a downpour of emotion.

She handed the phone to Anne.

"My name is Anne. I'm a friend of Eve's." Anne paused, listening to Torbin, then she went on. "She's going to be all right, but we could use some help. We're at Tenth and Broadway," she said, smiling at Eve as she gave Torbin the exact address.

Chapter Twenty

"Hi, I'm Richard."

"Hi, Richard," the group said enthusiastically.

"I'm an alcoholic, and I've been sober ninety days."

"Yea!" everyone cheered, smiling at Richard, who sat in the circle across from Eve.

"My father is an alcoholic. My mother is an alcoholic, and my two brothers are alcoholic. I'm trying to break the pattern"—he sighed—"but it isn't easy."

They all sat there, expectantly, giving Richard the time and the encouragement to say whatever it was he was trying to say, whatever was important to him that moment.

"I almost slipped last night," Richard went on, looking down at the floor. This was obviously very difficult for him. "But I called Anne. I guess I'm lucky. I know I'm lucky." He laughed.

Anne smiled encouragement at Richard.

"My mom was home last night. She'd been drinking by the time I got there, and she was in a foul mood 'cause she didn't know where my dad was. So she started picking on my brother—for nothing, really. He didn't answer her. He just said 'Here we go again' under his breath and walked out of the kitchen. I knew damn well where he was going. Right to his room to haul out a bottle so he wouldn't have to feel anything. Do anything. Right? But don't let yourself feel your feelings. I know the syndrome. I've been there too many times myself. So I tried to talk to her. I asked her why she always picks on Robby. I just wanted her to really think about it, but it wound up like it usually does, with her yelling and screaming at me, cussing me out for always taking Robby's side. So naturally I start feeling guilty again. Like she's had a tough time, and I'm only making it harder on her. And she starts telling me what she always tells me when she's drunk and she's mad at me.''

Richard coughed and paused for a long time, but no one hurried him along.

'' 'You were a damn accident,' she yells at me, 'and you've been causing me trouble all your life.' I know if she remembers what she said tomorrow, she'll try to make it up to me, but right then, at that moment last night, I suddenly realized—it really hit me like a ton of bricks—that there was nothing she could ever do in this life to make it up to me. And I swear to God, I got so depressed I just wanted to get to the bottom of a bottle as fast as I could and just wipe it out. All of it. Everything she said. And the pain, you know, the terrible pain.''

Everyone sat silently for a few moments. Then the woman who was leading the group looked at Richard and said, ''Thank you, Richard.''

And Richard thanked her back.

Eve raised her hand, and the facilitator acknowledged her. Eve didn't know exactly what she was going to say. Only that she had to say something. It was the first time she had ever spoken up at an Al-Anon meeting. At the other meetings when she had been asked if she wanted to share anything with the group, she had always said "no, thanks," but today she had to talk. She needed to tell Richard that she knew how he felt, even if she wasn't an alcoholic herself.

"Hi, I'm Eve."

"Hi, Eve," everyone said.

"I just want to respond to what Richard said. I—I know what it feels like. I mean, even though I'm not an alcoholic, my—my father is," she said, dripping with sweat, her hands shaking. "And I just wanted you to know that we all have our own bottles. Our own way of wiping out pain, of not feeling. But I guess we have to feel even if it hurts so bad we don't think we can survive it another minute. I learned that from Anne. Every time I thought things couldn't get worse, they did. It's still hard for me to talk about it. I guess I'm not ready for that yet, but I've learned a lot about myself in the past few months, and one of the things I learned is that I'm not alone."

Eve paused for a moment. Then she looked at Richard. "That's all I have to say, I guess. Except that you're not alone either."

She tried to concentrate for the rest of the meeting, but it was hard for her to keep her mind on what people were talking about even though she was interested. Each of them had something to say about a father or mother or sister or brother who was an alcoholic, and Eve heard bits and pieces of conversations, but it was only when it related directly to her that she really listened. She was still processing what Richard had said.

It was so clear to her that Richard wasn't responsible for his mother's behavior, but she couldn't quite transfer that to herself. She still felt guilty about her father's arrest. She felt guilty when she heard someone else ask, "How did I put myself in that situation?" Because she asked herself the same question over and over again. Had she set herself up by going to see her father without calling him first? Did she know, on some level, he would probably be drinking? Had she wanted the confrontation so she could finally and forever divest herself from him without feeling guilty?

There were still a lot of questions she had to answer for herself, but the good part was that at least she was asking them.

Anne came over to her afterward and slung an arm casually around her shoulder. Eve smiled at her. "Take a ride with me," Anne said.

"Where?"

"I'm going to an AA meeting."

"Another meeting?"

"AA—it's different," Anne said.

"Why are you going?"

"It's my regular group," Anne explained.

"I don't get it," Eve said.

"There's nothing to get. I'm an alcoholic," Anne said.

Eve just stared at her.

"Yeah," Anne said. "I'm a recovering alcoholic. I've been sober four years."

"You?"

"Me. Anybody can be an alcoholic, you know? One of your teachers, maybe, your doctor, the salesman or saleslady in the department store, the kid next door. Anybody can have the disease. Some of us want to get rid of it," she said, laughing. "I couldn't do it myself, even though you kids think I'm invincible."

"Why do you want me to go with you? Do you need support?"

"Sort of," Anne said enigmatically.

"Let's go, then," Eve said, opening the door for Anne.

* * *

"I'm Millie," the elegantly dressed, middle-aged lady said when she got up to speak in front of the group.

Eve liked her right away. There was an openness about her in spite of the fact that she was perfection itself. Straight and tall, blond and beautiful, every hair in place, every eyelash swept up with just enough mascara, every tooth shiny white.

"She looks like you," Anne whispered to Eve.

"Actually she does look a little like my mother." Eve sighed. "Only she's probably a lot more together," she said sadly.

"I'm an alcoholic," Millie said. I've been sober two years, and today is a special day for me. It's my two-year birthday."

Everyone clapped.

"Today," she said, choking up, "the two people who mean more to me than anything in the world are going to give me my cake."

She looked out into the audience. She was smiling, but her bottom lip was twitching. This was obviously an important moment for her. From the back of the room, a distinguished-looking man of about fifty and a young boy of about eight or nine came forward carrying a birthday cake with two candles.

"My husband, Lawrence, and my son, Perry," she said.

Everyone clapped.

Millie's husband and her son put the cake on the lectern and kissed and hugged Millie. "Thank you for standing by me," she said, tears falling down her cheeks.

Eve didn't know if the other people in the group felt as she did or not, but she knew if she didn't turn away from them, she wouldn't be able to keep from crying herself.

She looked down at her lap. Why was it that joy was sometimes as difficult as pain?

Her mind wandered in a dozen different directions, so she didn't see the man walk quickly down the aisle past her and head up the two steps to the platform, but she recognized his voice as soon as he began to speak. She wanted to run out of there as fast as she could. She started to get up, but Anne put her hand on Eve's arm. "Trust me," Anne said, and she nodded to the row in back of them. Stephanie and Torbin were sitting there.

Torbin put his hand on her shoulder.

She moved forward on her seat, ready to fly if it got too bad.

"I hit bottom two months ago," her father began.

Eve sunk back into her seat. He was going to say it publicly. He was going to tell everyone what he had done. Her father, of all people.

"This is very hard for me," he said. "I'm a private person. I don't like to hang my wash out in public, but there's something more important to me right now than my own pride."

Then he said it. He told them everything that had happened the day Eve came to the house unannounced, and he told them how the police had arrested him.

"By the time they got there, I had managed to drink myself into a total stupor. I wanted to black out so I wouldn't remember. I tried to pretend to myself I hadn't done what I had done, but I knew deep down that I had. By the time I stood in front of the judge, I was dead sober. I told her exactly what happened. And I told her to throw the book at me. I deserved to die for what I did. I wanted to die. The judge looked at me for a long time. Then she said, 'I don't think your dying would do anybody any good. But your living might.' Then she asked me if I was an alcoholic. For a minute I couldn't answer her because there was still some part of me that resisted, but I finally told her I was. 'I don't think your intention was to harm your daughter,' she said, 'but nevertheless you did. However, the court believes that you, in all sincerity, believed you were reaching out for your wife, so we will order you to attend AA meetings at least three times a week for the next year, and to see a family counselor.' "

Eve held her breath. She had no idea what her father was going to say next, but she didn't trust a word he said, no matter how sincere he sounded.

"I love my daughter very much," her father whispered hoarsely, "but I'm not going to ask for her forgiveness, or her sympathy—or her love. Not yet. But I am going to ask her if she'll present my cake to me on my first birthday, when I'm one year sober."

Everyone except Eve clapped as her father walked back into the audience. She was too numb to clap. She just wanted to sit there and think about what her father had said. Sure he had come a long way, but she was so afraid to see him. She hadn't even talked to him for two months, even though Anne had asked her several times if she wanted her to call so the three of them could get together.

She still didn't trust her feelings at the end of the meeting, and she was glad that her father was walking out the door and that he didn't expect her to say anything to him.

Stephanie gave her a hug and said she had to run. Anne said she was glad Eve had come, and she'd see her at the Al-Anon meeting next week, and Torbin just stood with his arms around her and held her.

Suddenly she broke loose and ran to her father, yelling, "Wait."

He turned around and walked back toward her. Neither of them reached out to the other, but both of their hands were clenched tightly at their sides.

"I'll do it. I'll present you your one-year cake," she said.

"Thanks," her father said.

"And I hope I can present your two- and three-year cakes too. And ten and twelve years."

"I'm sorry," her father said.

"I know that."

"I can't make this one up to you."

"You can stay sober."

"I really do love you."

"I'm not coming home."

"I know that."

"But maybe I can drop by, see you once in a while."

"I'd like that very much."

"We can pop open a few cans of Coke," Eve said, feeling shy.

"That's all we'll have in the house."

"I'll call first," she said, looking him in the eyes for the first time.

"You don't have to. It's your house too."

"Okay—so I'll see you."

"Okay."

Eve turned to walk away. She sensed Torbin standing there quietly behind her. Then she turned back to her father. He was still standing there, looking at her. She walked back to him and stood there for what seemed like a week. Then she reached out and quickly hugged him. "I love you too," she said quietly as she backed away.

"So, see you around, then," her father said, smiling at her.

"Yeah, see you around," Eve said, then she turned to Torbin and took his hand. They walked to his car with their arms around each other. It felt natural that way.

About the Author

Marilyn Levy, a former English teacher and children's TV writer, is married, has two daughters, and lives in Santa Monica, California.

Teens
learn to make tough
choices and the meaning of
responsibility in novels
by **Marilyn Levy**